THE 3RIDE OF DEMISE

3

Keishi Ayasato

Illustration by murakaruki

My name is Dawn Princess. My alias is Grand Guignol.

"Even if you don't want it, don't ask for it, don't accept it, I shall be by your side for all eternity."

Dawn Princess

Kou focused on his next words,
which he said with great care.
Even if he turned back time.
Even if these moments were erased.
He would never forget them.

The only path forward was that which led to battle.

"All right. Destroy them—as many as your strength allows."

THE 3RIDE OF DEMISE

3

Keishi Ayasato

Illustration by
murakaruki

YEN
ON

New York

THE BRIDE OF DEMISE

3

KEISHI AYASATO

Translation by Jordan Taylor
Cover art by murakaruki

SHUEN NO HANAYOME Vol.3
©Keishi Ayasato 2021
First published in Japan in 2021 by KADOKAWA CORPORATION, Tokyo.
English translation rights arranged with KADOKAWA CORPORATION, Tokyo through TUTTLE-MORI AGENCY, INC., Tokyo.
English translation © 2023 by Yen Press, LLC

Yen On
150 West 30th Street, 19th Floor
New York, NY 10001

Visit us at yenpress.com • facebook.com/yenpress • twitter.com/yenpress
yenpress.tumblr.com • instagram.com/yenpress

First Yen On Edition: February 2023
Edited by Yen On Editorial: Emma McClain
Designed by Yen Press Design: Andy Swist

Yen On is an imprint of Yen Press, LLC.
The Yen On name and logo are trademarks of Yen Press, LLC.

Library of Congress Cataloging-in-Publication Data
Names: Ayasato, Keishi, author. | Mura, Karuki, illustrator. | Taylor, Jordan (Translator), translator.
Title: The bride of demise / Keishi Ayasato ; illustration by murakaruki ; translation by Jordan Taylor.
Other titles: Shuen no hanayome. English
Description: New York, NY : Yen On, 2022.
Identifiers: LCCN 2022010509 | ISBN 9781975337940 (v. 1 ; trade paperback) | ISBN 9781975337964 (v. 2 ; trade paperback) | ISBN 9781975338015 (v. 3 ; trade paperback)
Subjects: LCGFT: Fantasy fiction. | Light novels.
Classification: LCC PL867.5.Y36 S4813 2022 | DDC 895.63/6—dc23/eng/20220311
LC record available at https://lccn.loc.gov/2022010509

ISBNs: 978-1-9753-3801-5 (paperback)
978-1-9753-3802-2 (ebook)

10 9 8 7 6 5 4 3 2 1

LSC-C

Printed in the United States of America

The Bride of Demise

|

Table
of
Contents

Cover and illustrations by murakaruki

PROLOGUE

Kou Kaguro opened his violet eyes.

An intense light seared his retinas.

Familiar Academy sights were now shrouded in flames. The buildings for every major had been destroyed, and rubble was strewn across the ground. Even the café and shops located inside the Academy had been ruined and burned beyond recognition.

Central Headquarters alone, with its winged silhouette, just barely managed to retain its dignity.

In the distance, Pandemonium was leading the other students in an evacuation. There weren't many people still alive. A great number had been killed in the first wave of destruction. Even now, Kou could see someone's arm poking out from beneath the rubble. The air was heavy with heat and thick with the scent of smoke and burning flesh.

Kou Kaguro stood, unmoving.

He simply stared at the kihei in front of him.

It looked like a girl.

She stood in the Academy's square, her wings spread. Those wings, nothing more than an odd framework made from what looked like bones, clashed with her sweet appearance. There was a flash of blue light and a harsh, grating sound of machinery operating. But then the wings folded away in the blink of an eye, completely gone, and returned to her body as if they'd never been there.

She slowly blinked, then looked toward Kou. She stretched out her hand, like she was asking him for something.

He didn't respond. Silently, he readied his sword.

A building somewhere crumbled, and the fire gathered strength.

Wreathed in dancing crimson flames, the girl lowered her gaze. Her lips slowly parted, and she said, "I wanted to be with you forever. I wanted to be by your side forever. But that wasn't enough… This is my resolve. This is the proof of my love. This is the twisted manifestation of my desire. This is my…my…"

There, her words faltered for a moment. Her wings flew open once again.

The resulting burst of wind swept through the encroaching flames, sending a ring of crimson rushing into the air.

Surrounded by that dreadful sight, the girl closed her eyes.

Like a prayer, she whispered, "…This is my dream. My name is Dawn Princess. My alias is Grand Guignol."

Just like a princess in a fairy tale, like a witch in a fable, the awoken girl made an oath.

"Even if you don't want it, don't ask for it, don't accept it, I shall be by your side for all eternity."

"…I refuse," came Kou's simple response.

The girl smiled as if she'd known he would say that. Her smile was tender, filled with childlike innocence.

She continued to smile as countless people died around them.

She looked beautiful and cruel, horrifying and comical. But most of all, she simply looked heart-achingly alone.

1. HANGING OUT WITH FRIENDS

【Memories from the Beginning of the End: Black Princess】

I think…part of me suspected it might happen, that it might turn out like this.

I don't particularly care, though. Our hardships will likely continue, but I don't lament that fact, nor does it bring me sorrow. I simply respect my Groom's decision. I find it agreeable. After all, my Groom is my light in the darkness. That is all that matters.

No matter what changes, one thing will always remain the same.
I will always love Kou Kaguro with all my heart.

So long as those feelings remain within me, I will follow him.
To heaven or to hell.

* * *

He felt like he'd been dreaming.
A dream about a time he couldn't place.
About a time he didn't want to be possible.
A dream drained of hope, a dream that should never be allowed to come true.

"Kou, are you awake?"

Kou Kaguro opened his violet eyes.

Someone's face entered his blurred vision.

Just then, a single tear ran down his cheek.

"...Huh, that's weird."

With a tilt of his head, he reached a hand up to his eye. Kou didn't usually cry. In fact, he had barely cried even as he went through hell fifteen thousand times. But now he couldn't stop.

He was baffled by the tears that flowed without reason. Before him, a blue-eyed girl similarly tilted her head in confusion.

"Kou, it's rare for you to cry. Did you have a bad dream?"

"Yeah... I did. I think it was the worst nightmare I've ever had." He held his head in his hands, trying desperately to remember fragments of the dream.

The Academy burning. Someone's corpse. Heat and the smell of burning flesh.

And a ridiculous yet sorrowful kihei.

But he couldn't remember much about that last part—the details still wouldn't come to him. Even so, a miserable, conflicted emotion churned deep within him.

He shook his head. His voice was grave as he said, "It was a dream I don't want to come true... That's the only thing I know for sure."

"It was that bad? Then I hope it wasn't a precognitive dream."

"I hope so, too," said Kou bitterly.

After all, he'd previously had just such a dream, foretelling future events. He could only pray that wasn't the case this time.

Can't believe I'm sitting here worrying about a dream...when I have so many other things on my plate.

His head ached as he looked around.

He was in the Central Headquarters' gardens. White Princess was kneeling on the grass in front of him, looking up at him with concern. As always, her eyes were like the sky, her white hair as beautiful as the snow.

From behind her, he could hear the sound of lively chatter he was now so used to. One after the other, familiar voices carried through the air toward him.

"Don't move, Black Princess. If you move, your hair will get all messed up."

"Th-that would be bad. Kou complimented my hair. I understand; I'll be perfectly still."

"Tsubaki, I feel like you're making way too big of a deal out of this. You're just putting a decoration in her hair."

The first voice was from a small blond girl named Tsubaki Kagerou, followed by that of Kou's second Bride, the black-eyed, black-haired beauty called Black Princess. The last voice came from a male student with androgynous features named Rui Yaguruma. He was standing firmly in place, making a fuss.

It appeared Tsubaki had managed to do Black Princess's glossy hair up in complex braids, and now she was carefully placing a hairpin with a flower ornament into her handiwork. Yaguruma was serving as her assistant, holding Black Princess's hair in place as Tsubaki worked. He looked fed up, but the girls were treating the process with utmost importance. Their expressions were as tense as if they were in the midst of combat.

As Kou watched them, two more voices joined in.

"It's because she's managed to do it up so nicely. I understand not wanting to ruin it now... Oh, by the way, Hikami, would you like some more tea?"

"Yes, please. Watching them like this makes me feel like a father on his day off."

"Which would make me the mother, I take it?"

"Ha-ha-ha! So we're a loving married couple? ...Uh, wait a second. That's an awful joke. No, it won't do, not at all."

The boy with an eye patch covering one eye was Ryuu Hikami, and the graceful girl with him was Mirei Tachibana. Their back-and-forth was like a honed performance designed to make everyone else impatient with them.

Actually, it seemed more like Hikami had simply self-destructed and was now anguishing over it all by himself. Mirei, on the other hand, coolly sipped her tea, unconcerned. As usual, one of her slender, elegant feet was pushing down on her Bride.

As the seven of them spent their break time in peace, Kou was busy thinking. Looking only at the brilliant scene before him, he might be tempted to believe there was nothing wrong in the world. But that wasn't the case.

He narrowed his eyes and thought back to the festival.

* * *

At the festival to celebrate making it through the Gloaming, a scheme drawn up by a few individuals high up in the school's leadership had led to Kou being stabbed to death over and over. Each time, the perpetrator had been one of his friends under mind control. He'd also had to face the deaths of many of the members of Pandemonium. It had been a total nightmare.

Kou had used his ability to travel back in time and managed to prevent the worst possible outcome. He had succeeded in striking down the one causing it all—the kihei with the alias Opening Ceremony, the lost number five of the Princess Series.

The lost number five was able to upset the magic inside living things, allowing her to manipulate both humans and other kihei. She had also been the one to cause the Gloaming, efficiently stirring up the magic gathered in the queen of the kihei and sending her on a rampage.

But she hadn't done any of that of her own volition. Humans had ordered it done. From this, it was clear the worst disaster known to humankind, the Gloaming, was indeed man-made. And yet...

I still don't know why, thought Kou.

According to Kagura, a possible goal might be to thin out the overgrown kihei population and to eliminate Pandemonium when they grew too powerful. But Kou felt the cost, in both lives lost and physical damages, was too high for such a purpose. For now, they couldn't be certain.

And above all...

I need to find out who wanted the Gloaming to happen and take them out.

It couldn't just be the higher-ups in the Academy. The Empire itself had to be in on it.

The lost number five, the kihei that had acted as the trigger of the Gloaming, was dead, but there had been no judgment rendered on any of the humans involved, even though their actions had resulted in countless deaths and destroyed so many students' lives. Kou couldn't let that go. But it was hard to ascertain who was pulling the strings, even with his special ability. Students couldn't go to the capital, nor could they interact with the Academy's higher-ups.

As a result, Kou's only choice was to leave it in Kagura's hands. And even then, there was only so much the man could investigate as a teacher. That meant Kagura's only choice was to use his power, a power that could shift the world out of phase, as a bargaining chip.

Kou clenched his fists tightly, keenly aware of his own helplessness.

Just then, someone pinched his cheeks and pulled.

"Wha ah you doing, Tsuwaki?"

"You looked out of it, so I pinched your cheeks."

"I can see dat mush."

"Wake up and look! We're finished," she announced, thrusting out her small chest with pride and causing her golden hair to sway.

There was movement behind her. Yaguruma appeared, looking like a butler as he held Black Princess's hand.

Black Princess seemed nervous; she walked forward stiffly.

Kou looked and saw her hair was decorated with an artificial purple flower. Her hair itself, which was normally pulled back in a single ponytail, had been worked into complex braids leading into a bun, showing off the pale nape of her neck.

It was a beautiful style, and also somewhat cute.

"Mm, that's very nice, Black Princess," said Kou. "It really suits you—both beautiful and sweet."

"Th-thank you, Kou. It makes me so happy when you compliment me. It feels like a warm ray of sun shining in my heart... I'll have to thank Tsubaki."

Black Princess turned bright red and brought a hand to her neck.

Kou told her again how cute she looked, which made her cheeks burn even brighter. She looked away and muttered something quickly.

Kou stroked her hair gently, trying not to ruin it, then said to Tsubaki, "I should thank you, too."

"Hee-hee, yes, be even more grateful. You can never say thank you too much."

"You know, I've thought this for a while, Kou," said Yaguruma. "Don't you think you're a bit quick to compliment the girls? It seems sinful. As your friend, it worries me."

"It's not like that, Yaguruma," replied Kou. "I'm just saying what I think."

"That's exactly what I mean." Yaguruma shrugged, fed up. Exasperation was evident in his androgynous features.

Kou tilted his head to the side, unable to comprehend what he was doing wrong.

Seeming satisfied with her work, Tsubaki began to climb up her rocky giant of a Bride, Doll's Guardian. She safely reached his shoulder and curled up there like a cat.

Suddenly, White Princess sprang to her feet and jogged over to Black Princess, practically dancing.

Black Princess hunched her shoulders slightly. After staring at her for a moment, White Princess gave a big nod. "Mm, yep. It really suits you, Black Princess. It's cute—but also beautiful."

"Y-you think so? Kou's compliment made me happy, but hearing you say so is just as nice. Thank you. You should have your hair done, too. If you like, we could get matching styles."

"Oh, that's a good idea. Then Kou can admire both of us... Tsubaki, I have a favor to ask. Could you do the same thing for me?"

"Of course. I'm coming down now; just a moment. Tsubaki's Beauty Parlor is open today only, but for now we're still here and receiving rave reviews. Your hair will make another wonderful canvas, White Princess."

Tsubaki descended to the lawn, guided by her Bride's arm, then beckoned White Princess over to the chair. White Princess nodded and sat in front of Tsubaki, who then started fiddling with her smooth silvery-white hair. Yaguruma served as assistant once again. Black Princess hovered near them, trying to see if there was anything she could do to help.

Kou sat down beside Hikami and Mirei as all three of them gazed at the scene with warmth in their eyes. At a snap of Hikami's fingers, Unknown appeared, and he proceeded to tenderly stroke his Bride's head.

"Kou, would you like another cup of tea?" Mirei offered with a smile.

"Yes, please."

Kou couldn't help thinking again how peaceful their current life was. If he became complacent, he might find himself lost in its sweetness.

To guard against that, every so often, Kou would recall the dark memories stored in his mind.

There was something only he, and no other student, knew: The Academy was absolutely not on their side. That much was certain. He couldn't let his guard down.

That said, there was yet another factor in Kou's life—a pleasant change—distracting him from all this and causing his vigilance to waver.

He could once again interact with his friends from the past.

* * *

"So…you're saying the super-secretive Kou Kaguro was late because he was too busy chatting with his other friends?"

"Sorry. I feel really bad about making you wait."

"Oh, come on, Isumi! You're being too critical. This is why you're not popular with the girls!"

"…It's not like I want random girls to like me anyway."

The three of them were in the Academy's café. Kou was seated across from Isumi Hiiragi and Asagiri Yuuki, his classmates from back when he was in the Department of Magic Research.

Asagiri blinked her large chestnut-colored eyes. The crease between Isumi's eyebrows deepened slightly. There were plates of dessert already in front of the two of them. Today's special was apparently a simple tart, and Kou had ordered the same thing.

Asagiri fiddled with her fork. When she noticed Kou looking in the direction of her tart, she hurriedly split it into large chunks, then stabbed one with the fork and held it out to Kou.

"Kou, open up!"

"Actually, I already ordered the same thing. Go ahead and eat yours."

"O-oh, right… You should've said something sooner."

For some reason, Asagiri's shoulders drooped in disappointment, and

Isumi, sitting beside her, looked grim. He seemed unhappy, but the glance he shot Kou held a bit of gentleness as well, as if he was saying "I know you've got it rough, too."

Isumi's dislike of Kou had softened since he'd learned of his survival. So much so that when he and Asagiri had agreed to meet regularly, Isumi had insisted he would join them.

It was Kou who had made it so the three of them could meet once again.

It had happened after the festival.

Kou had found Asagiri and Isumi and told them he was still alive.

Normally, it was best to avoid interacting with regular students, but Kagura had already given him permission so long as they stuck to chatting. *And yet...*, Kou thought bitterly.

While he had received permission, he'd also received a warning.

Kou thought back to Kagura's words.

"Opening Ceremony's ability was consistently activated at the end of the festival. But based on what you told me, Asagiri was the only one who stabbed you at an unrelated time.

"It was right after you told her about your Brides. Kou, I know you're aware, but I'm you, yeah?

"Sometimes, there's nothing so terrifying as love."

Nothing so terrifying as love?

That was true, and Kou was painfully aware of it. After all, that was the only thing that had kept him going as he went through hell fifteen thousand times. But Kou didn't think love was the reason Asagiri had stabbed him.

Besides, while this timeline's Asagiri hadn't experienced it, this was the same person who had thrown herself in front of Kou to shield him when Pandemonium was leaving the Academy, only to be stabbed by the regular students.

Kou owed her his life. Which is why when he contacted Isumi, he couldn't ignore Asagiri. He couldn't turn a cold shoulder toward the person who had died to save him.

To be honest, Kou couldn't see any sort of darkness in the girl in front of him that might lead her to stab someone. She was always so bright.

Kagura must be mistaken, thought Kou.

Eventually, his tart arrived. The waiter, wearing a uniform popular with the girls, placed the fancy plate in front of Kou.

"Eat up, Kou. It's delicious!" urged Asagiri.

"Yeah, I will." Kou took a bite. It wasn't nearly as good as Hikami's cooking, though it wasn't bad for something made from synthesized food produced by spirits.

No student, including Kou, was supposed to know what a dessert made with real ingredients tasted like.

For some reason, Asagiri was watching Kou's expression with joy. "I'm so glad you could come again today!" she said with a big smile. "I was shocked when I found out you were alive—and a little disappointed when I heard you'd changed departments, you know? But this is more than enough to make up for it!"

"Thanks," said Kou. "You're always so nice, Asagiri."

"No, I'm not. I'm just saying what I really think." Asagiri blushed and waved away the compliment with her hand, then offered him another happy smile.

Isumi was making another weird expression. He seemed a little worn-out.

Asagiri paid him no mind and continued in a bubbly voice, "So, Kou, how've you been lately? Anything interesting happen?"

"Oh, right, me..."

The class called Pandemonium didn't officially exist. Because its members had taken kihei, humanity's enemies, as their Brides, their class's existence had to be kept secret. Kou chose his words carefully and kept his description of his life vague.

Then Asagiri and Isumi told him about recent events in Research.

"So yeah, our group's research was successful... Oh, and then...! Hee-hee, Isumi's so funny. We were doing some experiments on a kihei carapace, and—"

"Stop it, Asagiri, you don't have to tell him that."

"Huh, well now I really want to hear."

"Don't even try it, Kou."

The three of them were having a perfectly normal conversation for a group of students. Occasionally, Kou smiled—a smile that had become more natural of late.

As he polished off his tart, he thought, *The way things are now, all those secrets just seem like bad dreams.*

But they were reality. Kou wouldn't forget. Though he'd undone it all, he alone had witnessed the deaths of so many of those close to him and seen the darkness lurking in the Academy.

It was like a prison made up of time already lost, and he imagined himself trapped inside, all alone.

* * *

"All right, see you next time! We've got to meet up again next week! I'm always thinking about you, Kou! Don't forget! It's a promise!"

Asagiri jumped up and down, waving at him endlessly, her hand moving from side to side in wide arcs.

Kou gave a small wave back, but Asagiri didn't leave. She apparently intended to watch him go. Kou waved again, then walked off.

There were a lot of people gathered in the square. Some were standing and chatting, some taking their phantom beasts for a walk, others practicing for the next parade, or enjoying various other activities.

Kou wove through the masses of people as he moved away, and eventually Asagiri disappeared on the other side of the crowd. Then he passed by a bookstore where students were standing in rows reading.

Suddenly, someone yanked him back by his collar.

"Huh?"

"Kou, come here."

Kou was pushed into the gap between the bookstore and the neighboring armory. He could easily have brushed the hand off his collar, but he decided to risk going along with it.

However, as this was one of the people who had stabbed him, albeit while under mind control, he kept up his guard.

"What's up, Isumi?" he asked. "Thought we just said good-bye."

"Shhh! Lower your voice. Asagiri's always watching like a hawk until she can't see you anymore. She might come after us if we're not careful. …Just hold on a sec. …Right, looks like she isn't coming."

The tension drained from Isumi's body, but the furrow always in his brow now formed an even deeper canyon. Kou looked at him in confusion, and Isumi hesitated.

For some time, he seemed to struggle internally. Then, at last, he asked, "What...is Asagiri to you?"

"She's my friend."

"I thought so... But...is that honestly all you see her as?"

"Yes..."

"Damn... Guess hers is one-sided, too."

For some reason, Isumi let out a heavy sigh. He covered his face and shook his head, his long hair swaying back and forth.

Then he looked up quickly and, with an incredibly serious expression, said, "I was wondering... Are you seeing someone?"

"I am..."

"You are?!"

"Yes, I am."

Kou's reply came readily as images of the Princesses appeared in his mind. He couldn't help worrying Isumi would criticize him, saying it's rich that a white mask like Kou would be dating someone, but his fears were unfounded. Isumi pumped his fist in celebration. The gesture seemed very unlike him.

Kou was growing even more confused.

Then Isumi clamped his hands onto Kou's shoulders. "That's perfect, then. In that case, I've got a favor to ask you."

"A favor? Sure... If it's something I can do."

"You won't need to do anything. I just need your help. I've been thinking it over for some time, but I still can't come up with a good way to pull it off."

Kou was completely baffled, but Isumi's eyes were locked on him, unwavering. It looked like he wouldn't take no for an answer.

Isumi drew in a deep breath, prepared himself, and confessed.

"I want to ask Asagiri out."

Isumi's plea for help was completely and totally serious, but Kou was the last person in the world he should be asking.

* * *

With Isumi's confession, Kou found the answer to several mysteries.

In one of the festival outcomes he'd experienced, when Pandemonium was breaking away from Central Headquarters, Isumi had shown up, chasing Asagiri. And another time during the festival, at the haunted house, he'd met Isumi right after meeting Asagiri.

A lovestruck Isumi had probably been following her out of concern, leading to both encounters. And perhaps that was why he had been so harsh toward Kou when he was still in Research. After all, Kou had always been close with Asagiri.

Apparently, Isumi's feelings toward her were serious. Since he'd been asked, Kou wanted to help Isumi if at all possible, but there was a major problem standing in the way.

Yes, Kou did have two beloved Brides, but he knew literally nothing about the intricacies of romance.

"So do any of you have any knowledge on the subject?" asked Kou.

"My doors are closed," replied Tsubaki.

"Don't ask me. I'm less qualified than you, for sure," said Yaguruma. "I'm willing to bet on it."

"I'm afraid I'll be no help...," Mirei added. "All I can teach you is how to love your Bride."

"Same here," chimed in Hikami.

Those were the responses he got from his friends in Pandemonium on the subject. They were in the courtyard, essentially saying the same thing, each with genuine confusion on their faces. As they'd admitted themselves, they were all equally useless.

Hikami's expression grew even more severe, and he crossed his arms. "Besides, we're students. We have both our studies and our duties to take care of. Isn't any love, other than the love for our Brides, unnecessary?"

"I can't believe you're the one saying that, Hikami."

"Tsubaki, why are you looking at me so coldly like that?"

Hikami complained she was being unfair, but no one came to his rescue.

With that, Kou determined his friends wouldn't be any help. He decided to try asking the Princesses next, but both shook their heads.

"All I know is how to love you, Kou," said White Princess. "I know absolutely nothing else—and don't care to."

"All I know is how to love you, Kou," said Black Princess. "I don't wish to understand any more—and won't try to."

Then they both clung tightly to his arms.

He was happy to receive the love of his Brides, but he was left with an entirely new problem. Kou Kaguro's hope of using someone else's knowledge to bolster his advice had been completely dashed.

So what should he do?

Maybe I should try asking Sasanoe, too...

Just as this reckless thought occurred to him, Kou received an unexpected message from a surprising source.

It was an invitation—from the Puppets.

For whatever reason, they had invited him to attend a tea party.

The Bride of Demise

2. TEA WITH THE PUPPETS

【Memories from the Beginning of the End: Hikami】

If you're asking if I saw this coming, then no, I didn't.

To be honest, I'm still pretty undecided. If you asked me if I'm truly happy with the situation, I'd say no. Our decision is wrong in many ways. But I also know it's the right decision. We're already outsiders anyway. There's no place I know of that would accept us. That's just how it is. Though, if you asked me if that made me sad, I'd say yes.

Anyway, the most important people to me are here.

My Bride, of course, is important to me. Unknown's the one I love above all else. And there's also my friends: Tsubaki, Yaguruma, Kou, White Princess, Black Princess, and…Mirei.

That's why I agreed with his decision.

That's all it took in the end.

I'm only human.

A pitiful little human.

* * *

Greetings, Pandemonium. We, the Puppets, humbly invite you to a tea party. This party will serve as both an opportunity for us to deepen our friendship

with such worthy rivals as yourselves and a chance to exchange information.
We would be honored by your presence should you accept our invitation.

Sincerely,
Touji Kurumada

Dang, Touji can be super formal. So basically, we want to improve our
relationship with you guys. We're going to bring a bunch of tasty teas and
treats, so I really hope you'll come.

See you,
Helze Kakitsubata

"...What do you think?" asked Kou.

"I think the probability it's a trap is low," said White Princess calmly.
"Their main work is assassination. There's not much point in sending a
warning letter."

Black Princess was beside her, her expression grim as she fiddled with
the sheets on the bed. Every once in a while, she'd glance at White
Princess or Kou, then go back to fiddling with the sheets.

They were in their room, sitting on their overly opulent bed.

The two invitations were set side by side on top of the sheets.

If they were to believe the signatures at the bottom, one of them was
from the katana-wielding boy, Touji, while the other was from Helze,
the girl with the needles. A further sheet listed the date, time, and location, and included the lipstick remnants of a kiss imprint.

With the papers spread out before her, White Princess looked troubled. "I think there's something to be gained from going," she said.
"I'm especially interested in the exchange of information."

"Yeah, good point. But what exactly are they planning?" Kou's face
was a mix of various emotions as he crossed his arms.

Kou had undone several of his interactions with the Puppets. In this
timeline, he had never even spoken directly with Helze Kakitsubata.

And yet they'd received these invitations despite that.

Kou pictured the beautiful girl who was always joking around. Helze
was a difficult person to trust, but he didn't think she would bother

setting such a crude trap. On top of that, the Puppets hadn't reported
to the higher-ups that they'd fought Hibiya—Pandemonium's second
teacher—in the middle of the night in Central Headquarters. That
alone made it difficult to simply consider them enemies.

But the Puppets tried to take White Princess.

That was the one point Kou couldn't get over. He looked at White
Princess. Her blue eyes stared back at him.

Kou had experienced hell over and over to save her. She was the most
important person to him. Just being his Bride was enough for her to fill
the hole in his heart. She was a lovely, open, and honest girl.

He would never hand her over to someone else. He thought back to
his fifteen thousand repetitions and clenched his fists.

His eyes were fierce, but White Princess returned his gaze with a
smile. Suddenly, she reached out her arms and wrapped them around
him. Her smooth hair brushed his cheek. Her arms firmly circled
around the back of his neck as she tried to console him.

Her hug was like that of an elder sister, a younger sister, and a lover.

She nodded, assuring him there was no need to worry. "I know their
goal was to take me away. You told me about that… But they couldn't
separate us, even in their wildest dreams. I will protect myself. And
both of me will protect you, my precious Kou."

"I'll protect White Princess, too," added Black Princess from her
side. "It would be difficult to use my full power in the middle of the
day while at the Academy, but…I don't think there will be a problem."

She touched Kou's shoulder, trying to encourage him as well.

Kou thought over the words of his beloved brides. "…You're right.
Thanks, you two."

"You don't need to thank us. I will always be your wings," said White
Princess.

"Me too…," said Black Princess. "I want to be with you at all times,
like a shadow, protecting the both of you."

White Princess slowly pulled away from Kou, before coming back
to squeeze him once more. He returned her embrace. After that, she
finally moved away. Next, she hugged Black Princess. The other girl
was caught off guard by this, but she returned the hug. They looked at
each other and smiled.

Then the three of them went over their thoughts about the invitation once more. At last, all three decided to accept.

But there was still something bothering Kou—something that hadn't been made clear.

"...How many of them will be coming?" He grimaced and looked at the invitation again.

All it said was *Pandemonium*. It didn't say how many people or who specifically was invited. Kou didn't think the Puppets would complain no matter who Kou brought with him. In fact, they'd probably laugh.

That's just the sort of people they were.

Kou considered taking his usual group, but Hikami's Bride wasn't specialized for combat. Yaguruma's Bride also couldn't use her full abilities inside the Academy. Most importantly, the others weren't aware of the Puppets' existence. Kou was hesitant to involve his friends in a situation they knew nothing about.

I need someone who's likely to have knowledge of the Puppets, someone who's reliable...

Kou's mind raced. Was there really someone that perfect? Well, he could think of a few candidates, but... After thinking long and hard, he came to a decision.

"I can't be sure they'll agree to come, but I might as well ask."

The Princesses looked at each other, both wondering who Kou had in mind.

And so Kou decided to play his most powerful card.

* * *

"I mean, we did write *Pandemonium*, but even I'm surprised you brought the whole Phantom Rank."

It was the day of the party, and Helze was blinking her bright, honey-colored eyes as she watched the others arrive. Kou caught hints of honest surprise in her voice.

Touji, on the other hand, was looking at them with a twinkle in his eye. He opened his arms wide and with a booming voice said, "If it isn't Sasanoe! And Shirai, and even Yurie... It's been a long time!"

"I didn't really want to see you, to be honest...," said Sasanoe flatly, his low voice coming from the other side of his crow mask. "But yeah, I guess it's been since your leader got into it with ours."

Crimson Princess was beside him, silent and looking just as unhappy as always. Yurie was beside her, seeming tired.

She yawned and waved. "It's been a while, Touji. Ummm, probably haven't seen you since Sister let loose punishing your leader. You seem well. That's good, that's good. I'm glad." She nodded, her eyes dreamy.

Yurie wasn't wearing her uniform at the moment. Instead, she was dressed in what looked like a nightgown covered in frills and lace. It made her look a bit like a princess in a fairy tale. Her Full Humanoid Bride, Sister, stood imposingly by her side, like a prince.

"Mm, you're right, it's been a long time," said a muscular boy— Shirai—his arms crossed. "Though I'm not sure it's best we meet again." His expression was stern. Beside him was his Special Type Bride, Nameless, whirling his amorphous body around however he pleased.

Hidden behind the other three Phantom Ranks, Kou couldn't stop a cold sweat from breaking out on his forehead.

"K-Kou, maybe we did go a little overboard with our invitations," said White Princess.

"I didn't think they'd all come…"

These were the strongest people in Pandemonium, the Phantom Rank. The three of them, along with their Brides, had an overwhelming presence.

That alone was enough to cast an air of tension over the tea party.

The event was being held in a corner of the gardens in Central Headquarters.

Not far from the area Kou and his friends went to for their breaks. The Puppets were trying to be considerate and choose a place that wouldn't put Pandemonium on edge. Other than Helze and Touji, the gunner girl, Nina, and the martial arts expert, Harusaki, were also in attendance.

These were the people Kou and the Princesses had fought against during his second encounter with the Puppets. It seemed the four of them made up some sort of team.

"Well, we can't just stand here cowering. Shall we get this tea party

rolling?" said Helze, clapping her hands in an attempt to dispel the tension. She took a step forward. Her honeyed hair swayed as she made a graceful bow. "Welcome, Pandemonium. My name is Helze Kakitsubata, and I'll be the host of this tea party. I've brought lots of tasty treats, so eat as much as you want."

She gestured toward the table as she spoke in a singsong voice.

Below the clear blue sky was an arrangement of various sweets and teas. The part about holding a "tea party" had been true, then.

Yurie's eyes shone, and she quickly moved over to the cupcakes, her hand stretching out toward the brightly colored treats. She grabbed a cupcake and, not even bothering to take a plate, began devouring it.

With frosting smeared around her mouth, she said, "Sister, this tastes wonderful!"

"Oh, geez! There's so much sugar in that, you can't just grab it! Your hands'll get all sticky. Here, wipe them on this." Nina rushed over, her ponytails bouncing, and handed Yurie a paper napkin.

But Yurie just stood there, unmoving. Finally, Nina took Yurie's pale hands and carefully wiped them clean. Despite her baby face, Nina was apparently the type who liked caring for others.

"There, now you're all clean. Oh no, you can't just grab another one the same way!"

"Hee-hee, but they're so yummy. Please wipe my hands again." Yurie smiled happily back at Nina.

Meanwhile, Shirai was facing Touji and Harusaki. In a low growl, he addressed the severe-looking warrior and the long-haired beauty. "Kou is Pandemonium's newest Phantom Rank, and we won't tolerate you trying anything with him. I would have to get serious if you did... Are you really telling me today is just a tea party?"

"There's no need to get suspicious, Shirai," said Touji. "When we launch a surprise attack, we do it right. We don't bring cake."

"Touji, I don't think that's the best way to put it," said Harusaki. "But...it's true. We'd do something completely different if we were aiming to take you by surprise. So you can trust us. And...by the way, Shirai, how's Shuu Hibiya doing?"

"Oh, Hibiya gathered up all the slackers who weren't listening to lectures and was whipping them into shape."

Their conversation continued, growing more jovial. Perhaps the warrior types just naturally got along.

That left Kou, Sasanoe, and the three Princesses. Helze stood before them. She flipped her hair, the same golden hue as her eyes, and said, "Let me introduce myself again... Nice to meet you, I'm Helze Kakitsubata. Not that this is the first time any of us have met. I met Kou, White Princess, and Black Princess in the middle of the night in Central Headquarters... How've you been since then?"

"Not bad...thanks to you guys. But uh, why are you singling us out?" replied Kou.

"Got a bit curious about you after our little run-in. We originally had orders to take White Princess, but they were retracted. I was thinking we should take the time to mingle."

"Retracted...?" Kou's eyes widened.

He hadn't been expecting to hear that. And while Sasanoe's expression didn't change, he, too, was listening intently to what Helze said.

At present, Pandemonium's power was at an all-time high.

They had survived the Gloaming, after all.

The result was that Kagura, already incredibly powerful, was in command of Sasanoe, Shirai, Yurie, and Kou. If they put their minds to it, they could threaten the government's control of the empire. Or that's what a portion of the higher-ups were worried about, at least. Some were set on capturing White Princess, while others planned to murder the members of Pandemonium.

What did it mean that they had retracted those orders?

Kou frowned. Helze gave a catlike grin and said, "That's good news, isn't it? You survived."

"But what's going on...? What happened?"

"Kagura happened. It was all Kagura," she said, nearly whispering the name. Her smile grew wider. "After the incident with Moriya and Iseult, Kagura officially declared he'd throw the world out of phase the next time someone touched Pandemonium. It'd be self-destruction on his part, but nobody can compete with that trump card of his. Which is why Pandemonium is being left in peace, for the first time in a while."

She clapped as if congratulating them, then walked over to the table and picked up several cookies, which she then passed to White Princess.

White Princess sniffed a cookie, then carefully nibbled the edge. Afterward, Black Princess and Crimson Princess followed suit. All three quietly munched their cookies.

Helze shrugged and pouted at their reactions, unamused. "They're not poisoned or anything. I told you, it's just a tea party... And while I did have some good news to share with you, I also wanted to ask you some things."

"Right, of course you want something in return. What's your question?"

Her voice low, Helze asked, "What are you?"

Kou's breath caught.

Helze's honey eyes narrowed, as if she was trying to ascertain his true nature.

* * *

Kou felt like the air had abruptly grown heavier.

Helze's eyes were filled with suspicion as she continued. "For starters, it's weird that Hibiya took such a big gamble on you. It makes me think you're not just a pawn who's good at fighting. And even now, you're hanging out with a group of assassins you only ran into once in the middle of the night, and you're not scared of us Puppets at all. It's almost like you already know us."

Kou gritted his teeth and cursed himself, realizing his mistake. From Kou's perspective, this was far from the first time he'd run into the Puppets, and he'd failed to show the expected wariness and tension. In reality, the Puppets should be nothing more to him than a group of assassins Kou and the Princesses barely knew. From their perspective, the Puppets were showing him their human side for the first time, but Kou had responded nonchalantly because he was already aware of it.

This was something Shuu Hibiya had previously pointed out, too. Kou's reactions were so unnatural that anyone with good intuition could pick up on it.

Helze blinked her honey-colored eyes, then moved closer to stare at

Kou's face. "…Kou Kaguro. What an interesting person. What in the world are—?"

"That's enough." A tense voice interrupted Helze's question.

Sasanoe stepped in front of Kou, his cloak fluttering. He moved to protect his underclassman like it was the most natural thing in the world.

White Princess and Black Princess followed suit. White Princess held out her right arm while Black Princess held out her left so that they crossed in front of Kou. They stood before him, hiding their Groom.

There was a sharp glint in Sasanoe's eyes from behind his crow mask. "Kou is a member of Pandemonium's Phantom Rank. That isn't information easily given up to outsiders. Or are we allies, Puppets?" Sasanoe placed a hand on the hilt of his sword. He wasn't showing open hostility, but his next question cut. "Do you now leaderless Puppets want to play?"

"I'll to have to say no thanks to that. As much as I enjoy fighting, I don't pick fights I know I'll lose. Though Touji and Harusaki might feel otherwise." Helze raised her hands and, waving them gently from side to side, took a step back.

Sasanoe's fingers slipped from his sword, and Crimson Princess, who had spread her wings moments earlier, folded them away.

Behind them, Kou bowed his head slightly, expressing his thanks to Sasanoe and Crimson Princess.

That was close. He couldn't afford to let too many people find out about his ability to go back in time.

Going forward, I'll have to make sure I don't let on that I recognize anyone I haven't met in this timeline.

"Mmm, well, I guess that settles it," said Helze as she stretched. "We'll just have a normal tea party, then." It seemed she'd given up on teasing out any valuable information.

She held out a number of sweets, urging everyone to partake. It was like she was practically pulling macarons, cakes, crepes, and tarts out of thin air.

Despite being overwhelmed, Kou accepted a plate.

At this point, the Puppets didn't have any orders relating to him and White Princess. That meant Helze wasn't his enemy.

But Sasanoe turned on his heel and barked, "If there's no other business, we're leaving."

"Wait. Touji and I are in the middle of seeing who's stronger," replied Shirai.

"I don't want to! I've only had five cupcakes!" cried Yurie.

Their responses were casual and lighthearted. Sasanoe must have been developing a headache because he pressed a hand to his forehead through his mask. Crimson Princess massaged his temples to soothe the pain.

Helze looked troubled by his reaction. She moved toward another table and picked something up. "I guess I have no choice. I was planning on leaving this particular activity for later, but I can't let you go now. Sorry, but... Hiyah!"

She then chucked something toward Sasanoe. His reaction was delayed because he'd been looking at Yurie. If the thing flying at him had been something dangerous, he would have dodged in time. But it wasn't, so he'd let his guard down.

Kou's eyes opened wide. Helze had thrown a pie packed high with whipped cream. It was the age-old pie in the face.

This must have been the special entertainment she'd prepared for the latter part of the tea party.

The pie splatted right onto Sasanoe's face and stuck there. He clenched his fists so hard his knuckles popped.

And thus, a pie-throwing demon was born.

The Bride of Demise

3. ASAGIRI'S CONFESSION

【Memories from the Beginning of the End: Mirei】

Did I think it would turn out like this? No, I had no idea.

Though, I doubt there's anyone who saw it coming. Definitely not Hikami. As sharp as he is, he can be pretty dull sometimes. If you'd like to know if I have regrets... I do. Though, when it comes down to it, the only things that are important to me are my Bride and my companions. I would have been happy just spending my days with My Kitty and my friends.

So long as I can do that, I'm fine with anything.

I know well that the scales of fate are not easily tipped.

If you want to protect what's important to you, you must give up something else.

He knows that more than anyone. I'm sure that's why he made this decision. And why I agreed—because there were so many things that were precious to me.

And yes.

In the end, that makes me a traitor to a great many innocents.

* * *

Two days after the tea party, Kou and Kagura stood face-to-face in the classroom. They were here for Pandemonium's regularly scheduled battle training.

Kagura stood nonchalantly in his uniform covered with medals and the coat he wore over it.

Then he disappeared. Even though Kagura was no longer in sight, Kou didn't make any unnecessary movements. With one of White Princess's feathers in hand, he focused his senses, searching for signs of Kagura's presence near him.

Kagura's arm reached in from the left. His fingers grasped for Kou's sword, trying to take it, but Kou evaded by a hair's breadth. He slashed upward, trying to cut Kagura's arm, but Kagura wasn't about to take a hit. His move to steal Kou's sword had been a feint.

Kagura left a single black feather floating in the air, then the feather exploded. The explosion was small, but it was strong enough to easily send chunks of Kou's flesh flying if he took a direct hit.

By the time it detonated, however, Kou had already jumped backward, escaping the blast.

Then came Kagura's second attack.

It was a kick that could shatter Kou's bones, and he just barely dodged it.

Kou lost his footing. At the same time, he reached out a hand.

"White Princess…"

"I know, Kou."

He took a second feather from her and plunged it into the floor. Using it as a pivot, he somersaulted through the air. Kagura's fist rushed through the space Kou had just occupied.

The dodge drew a stir from the audience.

"Not bad."

"Oh, wow. He's so in sync with his Bride. And his movements are unreal."

"I've thought this for a while, but when the heck did he get so strong?"

"Right?"

"Exactly."

A few people's voices were tinged with doubt. Kou frowned and wondered if he should have held back just a little bit. But then again, it would be bad if they found themselves in a tight situation and the other members of Pandemonium didn't know his true power.

Hiding his strength had more cons than pros.

He put on a straight face and tried to continue the fight, but Kagura suddenly stopped attacking.

"Right, that makes three attacks. Not that I was seriously trying to kill you, of course. You pass, for now," he said, cracking his neck.

That meant practice was over. Kou tried to catch his breath as he stood up straight and gave Kagura a deep bow. "Thank you very much."

"I expect you to be more serious next time, too." Kagura shooed Kou away, and Kou silently nodded. "Okay, neeext. Hmmm, I'll be pleased if *you* can last five seconds."

Kou wiped away the sweat on his forehead and returned to his seat by the Princesses. One pair of blue eyes and one of black greeted him.

"Good job, Kou. Your moves were excellent."

"Well done, Kou. I expected nothing less."

"Thanks," he replied, before letting out a little sigh.

White Princess sidled gently over to Kou's side, and Black Princess shifted gracefully closer to his other. They laid their heads on his shoulders, their hair tickling his skin. He stroked their heads, giving them equal attention.

As he did, he thought back to his combat practice. Just as he wasn't a match for Shuu Hibiya in close combat, he still wasn't able to land a decent hit on Kagura, even using the experience he gained during his fifteen thousand repetitions. That day's practice had gone well, but it wasn't guaranteed the same would happen next time.

And he was aware of something else.

Kou Kaguro's development is abnormal.

The students of Pandemonium didn't know about Kou's time-traveling abilities. The only reason they accepted him now without question was because of Pandemonium's own particular nature.

"We are the proud members of Pandemonium. We lie in the dark, spoken ill of by others. Our Brides and our skills are everything."

Another big factor was that the people who knew Kou well—like Hikami and the others—sensed that he had reasons for not telling them and decided not to push him about it.

But that day, there was an exception.

"I knew it. You're hiding your real capabilities, aren't you?"

"Ah!"

Kou gasped as a low voice addressed him. He looked up to see who it was and found Sasanoe. The other boy didn't normally come to class, but he'd shown up this time. Perhaps what happened the other day had something to do with it.

Kou was slow to react. Before he could say anything, Kou's Brides responded for him.

"There's no need for interrogation, Sasanoe."

"I can't turn a blind eye to such comments."

Both White Princess and Black Princess moved to stand up, but Sasanoe held up a hand to show he meant no harm. The two of them owed him for saving them in the past, as well. While they remained wary, the Princesses fell silent for the time being.

Sasanoe moved in close so the other students wouldn't hear and whispered, "I thought something was strange during the Gloaming. And ever since that day, your eyes have looked like those of a veteran soldier. I can only assume you've fought many battles in the meantime."

Kou wasn't able to reply at once. A poorly executed lie wouldn't work against someone like Sasanoe.

But Sasanoe didn't wait for Kou's response. "Then there's what Helze was talking about. It lent some credibility to my suspicions."

"Sasanoe, I—"

"You don't have to say anything. You are part of Pandemonium. There's no problem as long as you are useful," Sasanoe interjected. Then he said something Kou hadn't expected. "If you deem it necessary, use me, too."

"…Huh?"

"I imagine your abilities are fairly convenient… You are a Phantom Rank. We are those who lie in the dark to support Pandemonium and the Academy. Don't ever forget the pride that comes with that, Kou Kaguro."

His heels clicked on the ground as he walked away. With a swirl of his cloak, he was gone.

Kou gave a deep bow as he mulled over the advantages of what he'd just been offered.

If it came down to it, he could use Sasanoe. That was an incredibly powerful ace to have up his sleeve. Now he had two powerful cards in his hand: Kagura and Sasanoe. That was something to celebrate. And yet Kou bit his lip bitterly.

He thought back to the worst possible outcome of the festival.

Sasanoe... This Academy might not deserve your protection.

But Kou couldn't bring himself to tell Sasanoe that.

* * *

It was the day of Kou's next meeting with Asagiri and Isumi. His feet were heavy as he trudged toward the café.

Isumi had asked him to come up with an idea for how he could express his feelings to Asagiri, but Kou hadn't thought of anything. He'd told White Princess he loved her time and time again, but he had no idea how to express love to someone who didn't return his feelings.

His mind raced as he tried to think of an excuse for arriving empty-handed, but when he reached their agreed meeting place, he didn't see Isumi.

He saw only Asagiri, sitting there, biting her lip. For some reason, her expression was severe. Her chestnut-colored eyes gazed sharply into the distance. Her face was overflowing with anguish and stress.

Kou hesitated to call out to her, but she noticed him arrive before he could do anything else. She looked straight at him and said, "I asked Isumi not to come today...since we don't have time."

"...What do you mean, we don't have time?"

"Come on, Kou. I want you to follow me." She finished off her tea and stood, then took his hand.

Not wasting a moment, she left the café and wove her way through the crowd, quickly putting distance between them and the shop-lined square. It seemed she was trying to find somewhere isolated, without anyone else around.

...This is just like...

The day of the festival.

This was like a repeat of the time Asagiri stabbed him.

* * *

Eventually, Kou and Asagiri came out behind the Academy.

They were surrounded by gentle rolling hills covered in thousands of graves.

Each was a testament to someone's death, standing under a clear blue sky. This place was a communal cemetery to remember those who died in the Gloaming.

Asagiri bowed to a nearby grave, then turned back to face Kou.

The wind ruffled her brown hair. She opened her mouth, then closed it. Silence surrounded them; nothing stirred.

Eventually, Asagiri seemed to work up the courage to speak. Her lips parted, and with tears in her eyes, she said it.

"Kou, I like you. I love you, Kou Kaguro."

Her voice was filled with sadness.

The declaration of love had been sudden and sincere.

But as he listened, Kou recalled Kagura's words.

"Sometimes, there's nothing so terrifying as love."

Asagiri loved Kou Kaguro. That meant Kagura's guess had been correct.

My memories are like a curse, thought Kou.

Under normal circumstances, this confession of love should have been a sweet moment, but to Kou, it sounded like a death sentence. If everything about Kagura's prediction proved accurate, then Kou would be killed here.

"Opening Ceremony's ability was consistently activated at the end of the festival. But based on what you told me, Asagiri was the only one who stabbed you at an unrelated time—right after you told her about your Brides."

Kou reacted to Asagiri's confession by tensing up.

Tears were still in her eyes as she asked, "Are you going to say anything back?"

"Uh—"

"Should I take that as a no?"

"I'm sorry. I can't return your feelings."

"Because there's someone else you love?" Asagiri quickly slid her hand into her skirt pocket. Kou guessed she might draw a blade.

Asagiri wouldn't be able to stab him if he knew it was coming, but that didn't stop Kou's heart from aching at the thought of a friend swinging a knife at him. He'd made light of Asagiri during his fifteen thousand repetitions, but she was important to him—his very first friend.

Besides, he didn't understand her reasoning. Why would she stab someone simply because they didn't return her feelings?

Kou clenched his fists tight. "…Yes, there is someone," he said. "I'm sorry."

"Yeah… I thought so."

She appeared to grip something in her pocket tightly for a moment, but then she slowly drew out her hand. It was empty. Kou let out a sigh of relief.

Of course Asagiri wouldn't stab someone because of her love for them. That was absurd. He knew well how kind she was.

But then she asked something strange, her chestnut-colored eyes opened wide. "Is that person…White Princess? Why…are you dating a kihei?"

"What?" Kou froze.

What did she just say?

Her head cocked to the side with a strange, jerky motion, but her words poured out smoothly.

"Is it because you made a contract with her in the ruins and she saved you? Is it because she's strong? Is it because she's the seventh of the Princess Series? Is that why she's special to you? And why I'm not? It just seems so weird; I don't understand. I've loved you for so much longer. I wanted to be someone special to you. But because there's nothing special about me, you don't—"

"Asagiri, wait! Who told you these things?"

"It doesn't matter who! That's not the point!" she shouted. Her voice was so loud Kou could feel his eardrums vibrate.

The gentleness Kou had once thought of as a symbol of peace had vanished from the girl before him.

She bit her lip so hard she drew blood. Flecks of red flew as she repeated, "It should be me, it should be me, it should be me—"

"Calm down, Asagiri. I don't know who's been telling you what, but—"

"No, you don't understand. This is my decision." Her mouth suddenly clamped shut.

Silence fell around them.

She blinked her chestnut-colored eyes and shook her head. Then she gently murmured, "That's enough, Kou... I get it."

"You get what?"

"That's enough."

Her lips squeezed together, making the shrieks from before seem like a distant memory. She turned on her heel and walked off, her movements almost mechanical. For some reason, as he watched her slender back, Kou thought she looked terribly lonely.

He chased after her. He felt like there was something he had to say. He had to tell her that White Princess wasn't his Bride because she was the seventh member of the Princess Series or because she was powerful.

His love for White Princess was something deeper, something stronger. He didn't know why, but he felt like he had to say that.

But Asagiri whispered sharply, "Don't come any closer or I'll kill myself."

"Asagiri..."

"I have a knife, so stay back. Don't say anything else."

Kou could tell just by watching her from behind—if he moved any closer, she would probably slit her own throat. She would do the same if he tried to speak to her. In either case, Asagiri would become nothing more than a corpse. Kou couldn't bring himself to take another step toward her. He never wanted to see Asagiri die again.

Refusing to hear any more, she moved farther away.

Kou remained where she'd left him, alone.

* * *

The day after he parted ways with Asagiri, Kou was walking around near the Department of Magic Research.

He couldn't let too many people find out about his survival, but he was worried about Asagiri. She had known a lot of things about him she should never have been able to learn.

He had a bad feeling about all this. What's more, Asagiri's words had seemed to imply a strong resolve of some kind.

I can't leave Asagiri on her own.

After all, she was his precious friend. He was walking along, thinking about this, when he saw several Research students coming his way from the Department of Medicine. The majority of them were wrapped in bandages. Kou narrowed his eyes, trying to determine what had happened.

One of the people in the group looked up.

"…!"

The boy ran over without saying a word. He was probably trying to keep the others from finding out about Kou, in accordance with his wishes.

Silently, Isumi gripped Kou's arm. Then he rushed off, dragging Kou along. Kou's eyes narrowed as he looked at Isumi. He, too, smelled of blood.

Kou wondered again what had happened.

Eventually, once they'd moved away from Research, Isumi stopped. In a grave tone, he started to tell his story.

"Listen, Kou… While Research was collecting kihei remains, a Type B came at us."

"A Type B… Are you okay, Isumi?"

"Who cares about me! Anyway, the upperclassmen took up a defensive formation as we were running away. But then the formation fell apart. People just ran off, and Asagiri… She's—"

"Calm down, Isumi. What happened to Asagiri?"

"She's missing!"

Kou's eyes grew wide. Going missing in the ruins essentially meant death.

Isumi shook his head, his face filled with despair. His words were heavy. "We already contacted Combat, but she's been missing in the ruins this whole time. It's not like she can move around too much by herself… I… Dammit, what should I do?!"

Isumi clawed at his hair, fear and confusion swirling in his eyes.

Kou thought back to what Asagiri had said.

"That's enough."

Could Asagiri have disappeared on purpose? That would mean she'd killed herself.

Kou shook his head. This wasn't the time to be thinking such dreadful things. He had to do everything he could for Asagiri. Besides, there was still something bothering him about what she'd said.

Something weird is going on... I need to start investigating from the beginning.

There had to be someone Asagiri had interacted with, someone who gave her the information about Kou's Bride. That was the first thing Kou needed to figure out.

Isumi was in front of him, still falling apart. As Kou watched him, he decided to travel back in time. These two people were important to him. He couldn't abandon Isumi and Asagiri.

Kou closed his eyes and opened them again.

For a moment, the entire world was colored red. Behind the red veil was Isumi, exactly the same as the moment before.

"What...?"

A drop of metallic-tasting liquid fell from Kou's mouth. Then he coughed up a mass of blood before passing out.

The Bride of Demise

4. THE ABILITY'S LIMITS

【Memories from the Beginning of the End: Tsubaki】

I had a tiny inkling this might happen. I don't mean I knew exactly how it would go, but I knew someday we'd be in the way. I think I always knew that. Humans are uncute, unpleasant, and difficult to forgive. And from the beginning, I never had any interest in the fight against the kihei.

I was just here so I could live my life with Doll's Guardian.

That won't change, no matter where we are.

And that's why I didn't argue with his decision. I just agreed. That's all there is to it. I bet there's a lot of people who regret it or are still worrying about it. But I'm not looking back. It's better this way. This is fine. We should actually be proud of what we did.

We decided to leave them behind.

So the least we can do is walk our path with dignity.

* * *

Surrounded by darkness, Kou was lost in thought.

Asagiri Yuuki was a kind girl. She always gave an extra prayer for Kou that the worst-case scenario wouldn't happen while they were gathering materials for research. She had the modest dream of owning a phantom beast. In the past, Kou had shown so little emotion that others called him a white mask, but it didn't bother her. She stayed with him.

And then came the fateful day of their research mission on the outside, the day Kou and Asagiri were separated by death.

"Take care."

He gave a small quick wave as they parted for the last time.

The sight of the flower petals at the ceremony and Asagiri's smile crossed his mind briefly.

Yes, Kou should have died that day. Asagiri should have returned to her normal life, like nothing had happened.

And yet…

"That's enough."

Kou Kaguro opened his eyes.

Something white and something black entered his blurred vision. His two beautiful Brides stared at him. Both pairs of eyes—two as blue as a clear sky and two as black as night—were filled with concern.

Kou realized he was lying on a bed, the two of them watching over him.

"Where…?"

It looked like he'd been brought to his own room at some point. He shook his head and tried to sit up, but four slender arms immediately reached for him. Both Princesses pinned him to the bed, whispering in serious tones.

"Kou, you shouldn't get up yet. They said you were coughing up blood. Just stay still."

"White Princess is right, Kou. Don't push yourself; you're not a kihei. Humans are fragile."

"No… I'm fine. Anyway, what happened…?"

Kou's eyes dropped to his chest. His vermilion uniform was soaked with blood, the remnants of what he'd coughed up. His vision was still foggy, and his eyes ached.

It appeared that what had happened just before he lost consciousness had not been a dream, but reality.

Which meant what Isumi had said hadn't been a dream, either.

Kou pressed his hands to his aching eyes and said, "I have to go back in time as soon as I can…for Asagiri."

"Aaactually," came a casual voice from close by, "I think you should give up on going back, *for now*."

Kou jolted, and his eyes darted around the room. That's when he saw Kagura lying on the couch. The length of the furniture didn't match his height, and his legs were sticking half off the end into the air.

He raised one hand in greeting and continued in a tone as casual as you might use to say good morning. "Good thing a teacher from Medicine contacted me right away. Things might've really blown up if they'd looked too closely at your body. I wouldn't have been surprised if you'd ended up on a dissection table afterward… But anyway, I've got bad news. Looks like you've reached your operation limit."

"Operation limit…?" Kou frowned, a bad feeling growing at the back of his mind.

Kagura nodded and kicked his legs up and down like a child. Then, in a singsong voice, he said, "Your magic levels are normal. No damage to your eyes. As far as I can tell, you can still use your ability. But the stress will soon be overwhelming. There's no telling when it'll stop working."

"What do you m—?"

"Actually, I wouldn't have been surprised if you'd reached your limit long ago," said Kagura quietly. Kou gulped.

Kagura was his other self, so the man's words had a greater weight to them. He continued without hesitation.

"Originally, you were created to be a supplementary component to the seventh member of the Princess Series. That's why you were able to take on White Princess's ability and replicate it to a certain extent. The thing is, while you're not quite human, neither are you a kihei. You're nowhere near as tough."

Kou's head was spinning. He'd used that ability to make it through all sorts of situations. Losing that power would severely limit what he was capable of.

But Kagura, Kou's other self, told him the cruel truth of the matter. "We don't know when your eyes will burst or your organs rupture. Going forward, you should try to use your ability as little as possible… I heard about your friend going missing, but there should still be time for you to see what happens *here*. You should gather as much information as you possibly can, then make your move."

He leaped to his feet and walked over to Kou, the hem of his coat flapping. He looked down at him and with a slight smile said, "It scares you, doesn't it? Going back to being a normal human."

"......"

Glaring back at Kagura, Kou remembered something. Kagura had also lost his ability to go back in time. To be more accurate, he was rejected by this world and became unable to use it.

Kagura shrugged in response to Kou's glare. "Well, I may have lost my ability to go back in time, but I still have enough power to throw the world out of phase. So you know, it just sort of is what it is. I'm not sure how to feel about it."

He gave a careless smile and pointlessly fluttered the hem of his coat.

Kou shook his aching head. He was having a hard time accepting the truth, but he instinctually knew that Kagura was right. He couldn't bear the thought of recklessly going back now, only to find he couldn't change things and could no longer start over and try again.

The greatest advantage of Kou's ability was its information-gathering potential.

Besides, there's a chance Asagiri is still okay.

His only option right now was to look to the future.

Then Kagura took something from his coat pocket and tossed it on the bed. It was a rolled-up sheaf of papers.

Kou picked it up, his eyes narrowing. "What's this?"

"You want me to tell you what's written on it? A week ago, some students went missing while the Department of Combat was in the middle of making a Clean Zone. The whereabouts of the two girls are still unknown. Five days ago, a girl from the Department of Exploration went missing. Two days ago, another girl went missing from the same department. And now, Asagiri Yuuki."

"...That many?"

"A lot of people go missing in the ruins. But a string of cases like this, and all girls—it doesn't seem like a coincidence."

"You think there's some sort of motive behind it?"

"Possibly. But it's difficult to follow all the threads at once. What do you think you should do next, Kou?"

"First, I think I'll investigate the ruins." Kou's answer was textbook. If Asagiri was still alive, she was likely still in the ruins. And if they didn't find her, they might still learn something by investigating the scene. "I plan to check out the area where Asagiri went missing."

"Eh, it might be a boring line of inquiry, but it's appropriate. Considering the number of students who go missing every year, it's highly probable she just ended up in an accident... But I imagine you have some unfortunate information that makes you think otherwise." Kagura said, peering into Kou's face.

He was right. There were some odd circumstances surrounding Asagiri's disappearance. Kou thought back to her strange words and behavior when they'd last met.

He clenched his fists and said, "Asagiri had information about White Princess. Someone told her White Princess is my Bride. I don't know why—or how it's related to Asagiri going missing... But it's too suspicious to assume it's unrelated."

"I see. I'd like to believe it didn't come from anyone in Pandemonium. I think there's a good chance it's someone higher up. Don't expect too much, but I'll do some digging of my own."

"Thank you. Right now, there's not much I can do myself."

Kou was asking for help. With his current restrictions, he was just a student who was pretty good at fighting. And investigating the higher-ups was difficult even when he could use his ability.

He made a decision based on what he was capable of right now. "There are places in the ruins that the Department of Combat can't reach... I have to search there first."

"Kou, we're going with you, of course," chimed in White Princess. She reached out and gently touched Kou's cheek. She lovingly caressed the outline of his face as she whispered, "You are my gift, my nourishment, my master, my king, my servant, my joy. And my fate. I'm sure Black Princess feels the same. We love you. We won't let you go alone."

"Yes, we are always together... You promised we would be. I want to be with you forever."

The two Princesses spoke passionately. They must have been worried about him, injured as he was. They softly took his hands in theirs. Just like a knight swearing fealty to a princess, they ever so gently pressed their lips to his fingers.

With his hand still in hers, White Princess hesitated slightly before speaking. "I'm sorry, but…I'm a little relieved your ability is now limited. It means you don't have to go somewhere beyond my reach and suffer over and over… I will protect you. I won't let you be sad all alone."

There was determination in her voice. Kou felt that all the things only he remembered had been like sand piling on top of him. That must have made his Brides sad as well.

Beside him, Black Princess spoke. Her voice was low and heavy as she said, "…Kou, do you remember? I, too, can go back in time."

Her brief statement startled Kou, but she was right. Black Princess was who White Princess had become after her own fifteen thousand repetitions. She still had that ability. She shook her head, her glossy black hair rustling back and forth, and whispered.

"But my ability is currently sealed. I belong to you, Kou. I don't know what might befall us if I continue to manipulate fate as I see fit, so I will leave it up to you. But that means we will still have a chance even if you die, and I will use my power if you ask. Please don't forget that."

"…Thank you, White Princess, Black Princess… White Princess, please don't worry. We will always be together. And Black Princess, I don't want you to use your ability. I don't want to make you struggle against fate again, all alone… It's okay. I won't leave you two."

The words came from his heart. He kissed them on their fingers, returning their gesture.

And as he did, he considered the situation. Everything will be all right if they find Asagiri. And if they find her corpse…

Then it'll be reason to go back, even if it's dangerous.

Asagiri had protected Kou, died in his place during the worst possible outcome. It was his turn to save her.

He squeezed his Brides' hands. They nodded, accepting both his fear and his determination.

5. SEARCHING THE RUINS

【Memories from the Beginning of the End: Yaguruma】

...I never thought this would happen. But strangely, I don't regret anything.

Maybe because...I sort of knew. I knew we weren't welcome. I could kind of feel it. And at this point, what else could we do? That's how I feel, anyway.

...We can't fight somewhere we're not welcome.

...My beautiful Bride can't run in a place like that.

So I'm fine with it. If we're alive in a year...I might say something completely different. But right now, with things how they are, I'm fine with it. I don't blame him, and I don't think his decision is wrong. I just hope he sees it the same way himself.

Because I don't want him to suffer.

I mean, he's my friend. You never want your friends to suffer, right?

* * *

They were at the spot where Asagiri went missing. It was in a small ruin that hadn't even been named. The area around the ruin and the first basement level had been designated a Clean Zone, but that didn't extend to anything below.

Still, the kihei in the area wandered along predictable routes, appearing in the Clean Zone only rarely. What's more, the kihei here were all Type B, so it had been decided there would be no problems exploring around the ruin and down to the first basement level. Despite that, it was still dangerous compared to other ruins.

The Research students had acted rashly.

Maybe they got bold after surviving the Gloaming... Though, there's no point in blaming anyone now, thought Kou.

As he thought, Kou looked forward. Nearby were the skeletal remains of structures made from as-of-yet-unknown materials. Plants spread their sturdy roots across them, bringing a serenity to the scene. Sometimes they would even see a small animal.

After walking for a while, Kou's vision opened up. He'd stepped into a wide-open circular space. The roof that likely existed long ago had been blown off, leaving pillars here and there. Short grass grew over the ground.

It looked a lot like the place where Kou had run into the Special Type before. Of course it did—while the ruins varied in size and level of degradation, their structures were all largely the same.

Here they found the remains of a Type B kihei, left behind during the attack.

A graceful figure suddenly crouched before it. Mirei's long hair slid down as she tilted her head. She thought for a moment, then said, "It's unlikely Asagiri wandered outside. There's only so much she could do while wearing magic armor. If she took off her armor...and then left the Clean Zone, she would find herself in a dangerous area. She probably wouldn't survive. It's more likely she's still alive if she stayed here in this ruin... She would have gone deeper, looking for somewhere to hide. Let's assume that's what happened for now."

"Combat is always low on students," replied Hikami. "They probably only searched the Clean Zone and didn't bother with any floors below, since the probability of someone surviving drops drastically. But there's still hope, since only Type Bs inhabit this area...or so I'd like to believe."

He stretched his arms as if warming up for some exercise.

Beside him, Yaguruma nodded quietly. "To be honest, it's not very promising. But I hope she's still alive. I'm used to seeing dead bodies at this point, but that doesn't mean I want to see the body of my friend's friend."

Next to him, Tsubaki stood with her arms crossed. She tossed her golden hair back as her jade eyes sparkled. "Yaguruma's right. It's obvious how bad the odds are, but it's annoying to just give up. Let's do what we can."

"Uh... There's something I'd like to ask," said Kou, finally joining the conversation. Mirei, Hikami, Yaguruma, and Tsubaki all looked at him questioningly. Kou faced the group, gathered there as if it were the most natural thing in the world. "Why did you all come with me?"

"Why? Because you said you were skipping class to go look for your friend," said Mirei.

"You're our friend; of course we'd come along. Am I wrong?" asked Hikami.

"I'm not so cold a person that I could hear that and just leave you to it," said Yaguruma.

"Kou, you don't rely on people enough. That makes you a huge idiot," said Tsubaki.

Each of them gave their own response, but the truth was that Pandemonium hadn't been given orders to join the search. Classes were being held at the Academy just like every other day. They might receive an order to move out at any moment.

And while Kou did need the help, he hadn't wanted to drag his friends into this. And yet they'd come anyway. Sasanoe was currently away at another ruin, but if he hadn't been, he might have lent his strength as well.

The support of his friends warmed Kou's heart. "Thanks, everyone. I'm glad you're here," he said humbly.

Mirei smiled, Hikami nodded, Yaguruma hid his mouth, and Tsubaki puffed her chest out in pride.

White Princess and Black Princess stepped forward, too. They gave graceful bows to the others.

"It's very reassuring to have everyone here," said White Princess. "As Kou's Bride, I, too, thank you."

"Thank you, everyone," said Black Princess. "As Kou's Bride, I am really, truly happy... Thank you."

Hearing this, the others couldn't help but blush. Mirei and Hikami glanced at each other, embarrassed. Yaguruma pulled the cloth on his face even higher up over his mouth. Tsubaki puffed up even further with pride.

Then Mirei cleared her throat and changed the topic. "Okay, shall we go then? ...As we discussed earlier, there shouldn't be any powerful kihei in this ruin. To start, we'll split up to cover the first basement level... We should be cautious when we move deeper. Hikami, as the weakest, will go with Kou, and Yaguruma will come with me since he doesn't have much battle experience."

Kou and the others nodded in agreement.

Then they moved away from the open area and into the ruin proper.

* * *

As expected, there were no kihei on the first floor.

They searched carefully for any signs of Asagiri but didn't find any clues.

"...Nothing really stands out, does it?" said Yaguruma.

"Combat *did* search this area already. Let's move on to the second basement," replied Hikami.

They regrouped, and all five of them, plus their Brides, descended to the level below.

"Hmm, the atmosphere down here really is different," murmured Mirei uncomfortably.

As they moved down the stairs, the air grew thicker and the darkness heavier. As if in response, the number of blue-glowing walls increased, keeping them from tripping in the dark.

They split into groups and proceeded. Kou and Hikami continued their search, but everything around them looked the same.

"I don't see any sign of Asagiri—or any broken pieces of magic armor," said Hikami.

"There's no trace of her passing through, either," said Kou.

As the two of them spoke, a loud shout rang through the ruin's halls.

"Everyone, come here!"

It was Tsubaki.

Hikami and Kou glanced at each other, wondering if she was in danger, then immediately dashed off. Their feet pounded the floor as they headed in the direction of the voice, all the while staying wary of kihei.

Eventually, everyone reached Tsubaki, but it didn't look like anything had happened to her. Her arms were crossed, and she simply stood, unperturbed.

Hikami frowned and issued her a warning. "Tsubaki, I don't recommend shouting while inside the ruins."

"I had a good reason. Look at this," she said.

Kou and the others looked down at her feet. There, they saw splashes of synthetic blood and scattered mechanical parts. In the center was a collapsed beast-shaped Type B kihei. Its head was crushed in, like it had taken a direct hit from Doll's Guardian. It looked like Tsubaki ran into the kihei and finished it off herself.

She shook her head in annoyance. "Who cares about that? This is what you should be looking at." She pointed straight ahead at the wall. The others looked and saw that a portion of it had collapsed. "See, a new hole leading to the side. Looks like it goes pretty far back."

"Oh...yeah... It looks like this isn't recorded on Exploration's records. It must have collapsed recently. It would be a good idea to investigate. There's a chance Asagiri might have jumped in there if she ran into a Type B," said Hikami, and Kou nodded.

Kou had actually done something similar, diving into a side tunnel in an attempt to throw off the Special Type kihei pursuing him. They couldn't rule out the possibility that Asagiri had done the same.

"We don't know what's waiting for us in there. I'll go," said Hikami.

"Hold on. When I went into a hole like this before, there was another hole in the ground that dropped into the floor below. It'd be dangerous if you fell, so I'll go," said Kou.

"And I, Kou's wings, will go, too."

"And me, of course."

The Princesses readily volunteered. Kou nodded firmly toward his Brides. Hikami was convinced as well. White Princess entered the hole first, then Kou, with Black Princess taking up the rear.

Their friends watched as they squeezed into the hole. For a while, they crawled on through the tight space.

White Princess looked ahead and said, "It doesn't look like there are any holes in the ground ahead. I will continue moving."

"White Princess, don't let your guard down."

"The rear is also clear. Let's continue," said Black Princess.

The three of them called out to each other as they moved. The darkness stretched on ahead, blotting everything from sight.

Then, all at once, Kou and the Princesses found themselves in a brightly lit space.

"This place…is huge… Uh, Kou!"

"What's wrong, White Princess?! What…in the…?"

"…I don't know what this is, either. What is happening to the kihei?"

The three of them emerged from the hole, then stood dumbfounded, whispering to one another.

A strange scene lay before them. The room was large, the size of a concert hall, but the truly weird part was what was on the walls.

Every inch of them was covered with incubation nests.

* * *

Incubation nests were pieces of equipment that propagated kihei.

They were translucent and vaguely resembled a human womb. Each one was set into a honeycomb-shaped case, and the insides were filled with a nurturing fluid. Kihei would regularly deconstruct their own bodies and place the parts in the nest, which would allow new kihei to be born.

Students had a responsibility to destroy incubation nests on sight and to gather a sample from them if possible.

However, the case housing the incubation nests was incredibly hard. A student would be unable to do so much as scratch it, and that was true even if they were wearing magic armor.

But Pandemonium was different. It was easy for them to eliminate the nests, to destroy and even to take samples from them.

But the ones in front of Kou and his Brides were unusual.

It feels like we're inside a beehive.

Standing there, Kou grew dizzy. The hexagonal cases were lined up in rows along the massive walls. Inside each one, large numbers of kihei parts floated in nurturing fluid. Kou looked at the bubbling honey-colored liquid and thought.

The room almost seemed like a laboratory.

Taking in the situation around him, Kou came to a conclusion.

This must be the site of abnormal kihei propagation. It was as if the kihei had been overtaken by a compulsion to increase their numbers.

The three of them were completely caught off guard by the bizarre sight, but they couldn't afford to be distracted.

Suddenly, their ears picked up a disturbing sound. There was a rustling as something scurried across the floor toward them.

"…White Princess."

"I know, Kou."

He took one of her feathers and readied it without a moment's hesitation. Then he stared at the space before him.

Dozens of tiny kihei crawled across the floor. They moved sluggishly toward Kou and the Princesses like a swarm of caterpillars. The majority of them looked like insects, but something was strange about them.

Their legs were stuck on in random places. Some had heads protruding out from their side, some with eyes, some without. None of them looked like a regular kihei.

This had to be a side effect of abnormal propagation.

The speed of formation prevented them from maintaining their original forms through the development process. Resembling neither Type As nor Special Types, these "Children" closed in on Kou and the Princesses.

"So we must fight. I suppose I don't need to hold back this time," murmured Black Princess. There was only Kou and the Princesses here right now—and no risk of regular students overseeing what happened.

Black Princess's appearance instantly transformed. Her student uniform changed into her sensual jet-black dress. Crow-like wings bound with chains grew from her back.

It was the form she had taken when she was queen of the kihei.

She undid the chains binding her. The silver rings sprang back, dissolving into the air. She slowly opened her soft jet-black wings.

Beside her, White Princess spread her sharp, mechanical wings. "I give you my control, my servitude, my trust… This I swear, Kou: I will kill everything for you."

Her declaration rang out through the room.

As the Children approached, they made a rustling, mechanical sound.

White Princess and Black Princess both raised a hand at the same time.

"To try to touch my fate, my Groom—what insolence."

"I won't let you lay a finger on the one I love."

Blue and black light flashed at the same time.

A line burned through the Children and exploded. But the next wave appeared over the corpses of the first. These malformed kihei of abnormal birth simply marched blindly forward.

The waves of Children came without end.

Kou felt a shiver run down his spine. "How many of them are there?" he asked.

Something was clearly wrong with this situation.

The Princesses attacked with greater force. Black and blue light flashed in succession, cutting through the Children again and again. There was a chain of explosions. Mechanical parts flew through the air. A roar echoed through the hall, then died down.

Just then, Kou was struck with fear. It was unlikely what they were witnessing was confined to this ruin. There was a possibility this was happening, in secret, in all of them.

Something was changing the kihei. But if so, what was it?

There was one obvious possible trigger: the Gloaming.

This last Gloaming ended quickly. Student fatalities were kept to a minimum, which meant the kihei suffered fewer casualties as well... Afterward, they multiplied... Did exceeding a certain total number cause some sort of change in their overall behavior?

Some animals and insects are said to become suicidal when their population gets too high. But the kihei were doing the opposite.

Kou couldn't understand what this meant. He racked his brain as he swung his sword upward, before bringing it down to slice the Children approaching him in half.

* * *

Exterminating the Children didn't take too long.

Masses of corpses had fallen to the ground at their feet. Damaged kihei components formed piles, the synthetic blood still fresh as it pooled and spread.

But a new wave might arrive at any moment. They needed to hurry up and destroy the incubation nests.

"Let's end it here," said White Princess.

"Yes, it looks like we've gotten rid of them for the moment," said Black Princess.

The two Princesses took aim and unleashed beams of blue and black light. But nothing changed.

A few seconds later, they realized that the incubation nests had survived the blast.

"Huh?"

"What in the—?"

The two Princesses gasped in shock. Kou was at a loss for words. They'd never seen incubation nests this strong.

"Hah!"

"Argh!"

White Princess slashed out with a mechanical wing. Black Princess fired a volley of feathers like buckshot. The two Brides continued their attempts to destroy the nests, but even their most vicious attacks didn't leave a scratch.

The hexagonal cases remained, undisturbed.

The three of them were at a loss as they stared at the walls filled with incubation nests.

The Bride of Demise

6. FIGHTING CHILDREN

【Memories from the Beginning of the End: Sasanoe】

...Did I see this coming? How the hell could I?

I'll say this much: This is all wrong. I won't accept it. But I'm not going to force my decision on the others.

Anyone who's lost their pride should just leave. I won't chase them down.

That's all there is to it.
I have nothing else to say.

* * *

"Okay... This is definitely strange," groaned Hikami.

Everyone else was now gathered in front of the incubation nests.

Just as Kou and the Princesses were stumped about what to do next, their companions emerged from the hole. While they hadn't been able to hear the sounds of combat outside, they were concerned with how long Kou and the Princesses were taking, so they came after them.

Faced with the strange sight, the others, too, were struck silent. Once Kou explained the situation to them, they began to experiment with different ways to destroy the nests.

Tsubaki and Yaguruma were in front of Hikami, having their Brides attack the nests. Doll's Guardian swung his burly arms, and Fire Horse rushed around the area to her heart's content.

But just as before, nothing happened. The two narrowed their eyes and glared up at the nests.

"They're strong against physical attacks, too," said Tsubaki. "They didn't budge an inch when Doll's Guardian hit them."

"Fire's no good, either," added Yaguruma. "I'd hoped it would work, but not even Fire Horse's heat made a difference."

Kou's shoulders slumped in disappointment. He'd been particularly hopeful that Yaguruma and his Fire Horse could do something, but even her flames had little effect. The nests repelled all their attacks.

Mirei stroked the surface of one of the hexagonal cases. Looking at the parts floating inside, she said, "Let's withdraw for now and call on Kagura… We should report the abnormal propagation. If, on the off chance, this same thing is happening in the other ruins…then we need to do something fast. Otherwise, we may be too late."

Everyone else agreed.

Leaving these nests alone would result in a second wave of Children being born, which would increase the danger level of this ruin. It was no longer an option to wander around searching.

They needed to take this information back immediately.

Kou bit down hard on his lip. They hadn't found Asagiri, and now things had taken an extreme turn. The only positive was that they hadn't found her body in this strange room, either.

If Asagiri had gone into that side tunnel, she absolutely would have died.

In this situation, I can't force my wishes on the others and say I want to continue searching… If the kihei keep multiplying at this rate, they're going to form a threat even greater than the Gloaming.

He clenched his fists, trying to convince himself. He just had to keep believing Asagiri was okay.

Hikami unfolded his arms and took charge of the party. "All right, let's head back. Unfortunately, the search for Asagiri—"

Just then, they heard a strange, mechanical clunk.

Everyone looked farther back into the room. An unnatural gloom pooled there. Something had been sitting in the gloom, and now it slowly raised itself up, accompanied by the sound of whirring machinery.

Kou immediately realized what was happening.

Those Children weren't mistakes.

They were parts for something else—preassembled parts.

Countless Children merged together into a strange form. Then the massive newborn cried out—the sound like a roar.

* * *

Its form wasn't like a Type B, a Type A, a Special Type, or even a Full Humanoid. If it had to be categorized, it was closest to a Humanoid, but the surface of the "Baby's" body wasn't covered in synthetic skin. Instead, countless legs sprouted from all over it. Its hands had no fingers. Instead, blades of all shapes and sizes were haphazardly stuck to its limbs.

It had many eyes—too many. They sparkled, red and glassy.

Its odd form was difficult to describe, but its overall shape was that of a baby. It was like a grotesque parody of a human body.

One thing was clear, above all else: This creature saw Kou and the others as its enemy.

Pandemonium was used to sudden attacks, however. None of them showed signs of shock despite finding themselves in font of this strange, massive opponent. All Grooms and Brides immediately readied themselves for combat.

"All Brides in front. Tsubaki, be ready to create shields," ordered Hikami sharply.

The Brides formed a line before the enemy, with all Grooms behind them ready to give appropriate orders. None of them hesitated as they prepared to fight the strange creature.

Just then, two clear voices rang out. "The target is large. We'll attack first."

"Yes, it should be easy so long as we can hit it."

White Princess and Black Princess made the first move, releasing flashes of blue and black light. Their aim was true. The two attacks hit the Baby, but the light was reflected back.

"What?!" White Princess cried out in surprise.

Black Princess murmured, "So the creatures on its surface have resistance to light beams, hm? How frustrating."

The reflected beams scattered, headed right back at them.

Seeing this, Tsubaki cried sharply, "Come together! The attacks' power was weakened; I should be able to manage!"

She used Doll's Guardian to form a wall, blocking the bouncing light. The Princesses thanked her, and she gave a curt nod.

Meanwhile, the Baby moved toward them. Its metal arms gouged into the ground.

Before its warped hands could reach them, Mirei whispered, "My Kitty, it's your turn now."

The chains binding every inch of My Kitty's body fell away, and Mirei's Full Humanoid Bride stepped out from his constraints. He had regained his original, beautiful form.

Now free, he rushed froward. As he passed White Princess, he took a feather from her wing. With this superior weapon in hand, he picked up his pace.

The Baby swung its arms, but My Kitty leaped onto its mechanical knee before it could crush him. From there, he ran up the Baby's body, all the way to its shoulder, and readied White Princess's feather to strike. He used it almost like a needle to pierce the connection between the Children making up the Baby's structure.

There was a crash, then an earsplitting screech of metal against metal as one of the Children fell off. This created a hole in the Baby's shoulder, but the damage was minimal. The Baby didn't actually look like it'd been hurt at all. It swung its arms in great arcs, nearly smashing My Kitty.

Just before the attack landed, however, My Kitty leaped like a dancer into the air and off the Baby, pulling back.

That's when Hikami spoke. "There's no point just peeling off bits of the periphery. Its core is in its torso. There should be one part that doesn't move at all, holding it together. The combination of kihei is unstable. It should collapse if we remove the core." He pressed a hand to his head as he spoke. He was using Unknown's vision, from all its various parts, to analyze the situation.

His orders were precise, and everyone nodded. Kou, however, looked at the Baby, doubtful. *It won't be easy to pull that off,* he thought.

The Baby let out a cry, and the distorted mechanical sound overwhelmed everything else.

* * *

First...

Kou's eyes met Yaguruma's.

The latter gave a quick nod of understanding and pulled down the cloth covering his mouth. His voice was smooth and melodic as he whispered, "Go, my Bride, commander of flames. You always race with such beauty."

Fire Horse responded to the praise with a whinny before galloping off, her mane aflame. She circled the Baby, leaving a blazing trail behind her. Over and over, she scorched the Baby's periphery with her fiery hot flames.

Several of the Children's legs melted, changing into a viscous fluid that resembled red melted candy.

With this, Fire Horse drew the Baby's attention. It let out another loud cry.

Meanwhile, White Princess flew through the air. She cut across the space, quickly closing in on the Baby. Using one of her mechanical wings, she tried to slice through its torso, but the Baby brought its arms down before she could. It looked like the Children covering the surface of its arms had the same characteristics as certain high-level, shielded Type A kihei and were tougher than the others. White Princess's wings could easily cut through even a Special Type kihei, but her most recent attack had barely left a scratch.

"Another cut might take off the arm, though," said White Princess as she prepared to attack once more.

The Baby suddenly spread its arms wide. The gust from the motion slammed into White Princess and sent her spiraling through the air, until Black Princess caught her.

"That was close, White Princess," she said.

"Sorry about that, Black Princess."

"No need to apologize. It's my turn now."

She released countless black feathers from her wings, which flew through the air like bullets. Their sheer speed allowed them to strike the baby's torso, opening several cracks in its central parts. But it wasn't enough to destroy it.

The Baby reached for Black Princess, its massive palm bearing down on her.

The next moment, Kou, holding a feather from White Princess's wing, and My Kitty leaped at the Baby's chest.

"——!"

"Got it!"

The magic within the two blades was fire and ice. They crossed the weapons and plunged them into the cracks in the Baby's chest. There was a violent reaction, and the resulting explosion collapsed the Baby's central parts, causing it to lose its balance.

The Children started to detach from its body, clattering unceremoniously to the ground where they flailed clumsily. Kou and the others quickly and precisely finished off the ones whose underbellies were showing.

The collapse continued. They wouldn't be able to merge a second time. Just a few more moments, and the Baby would no longer be able to maintain its shape.

And that's when it happened.

"Everyone, fall back!" shouted Tsubaki suddenly.

In that moment, Kou realized something. As the one in charge of defense, only she had correctly read the situation and spotted the danger.

Only the Baby's head and the area around it remained. The inside of its throat was slowly being coated with a red color. As they watched, it grew hotter and brighter.

"It must be self-destructing!" shouted Mirei.

Everyone rushed to put distance between themselves and the Baby. Hikami immediately threw himself in front of Mirei. White Princess and Black Princess spread their wings to guard Kou.

But they didn't quite make it.

The next moment, the Baby exploded like a grenade.

* * *

To Kou, it seemed he lost consciousness for only a moment. Opening his eyes, he slowly sat up.

"…U-ugh."

He touched his hands to his joints. His body ached. It looked like the explosion had blown him across the room, but he wasn't bleeding; he was barely even wounded. He wondered why.

That blast should've done a lot worse.

That was when he heard it.

Hikami's pained voice. "Tsubaki… Hold on, Tsubaki!"

"How…? Why?" whispered Mirei weakly. "She should have protected herself first."

Kou's head snapped up, and he took in the horrible situation.

Mirei was squeezing a tiny blood-covered hand. Hikami, too. White Princess sat beside them. Blue light glowed around her. It looked like she was using her nanobots.

In the center was Tsubaki, collapsed on the ground.

Kou immediately understood what had happened. Tsubaki had protected all of them with Doll's Guardian's walls. In exchange, she had neglected her own defense.

"Tsubaki!" Kou stood up and ran over to her. He looked her up and down, then gulped. There was a huge shard of metal embedded in her abdomen. It jerked up and down every time she breathed.

"White Princess, how is she?" he asked.

White Princess was capable of healing even the worst of injuries. She'd once managed to save him even after he'd died.

But this time, she looked uncertain. She bit her lip. "The metal fragment is lodged deep inside her. I would need to take it out to heal her, but…there's a high probability she'll die the moment I do. I was able to resuscitate you, Kou. In the same way, I could kill her first and then treat her, but…there's no guarantee I can bring back someone who isn't my synchronized Groom… I don't know what to do. Kou, Tsubaki, I'm sorry…"

She hung her head, still working to keep Tsubaki alive as she apologized.

Kou gritted his teeth. Would they be able to carry Tsubaki back to the Academy with the metal shard still in her? No, the risk was too high. And it would take too long to leave White Princess here with one group, while the rest went back for help.

All at once, he was keenly aware of his own powerlessness. Tsubaki was struggling painfully to breathe, her face contorted in agony.

...Should I go back in time now? To before the Baby exploded... No, further, to before Asagiri disappeared...

He seriously considered these options as he watched the tragedy unfolding in front of him. Right now, Tsubaki was suffering. He couldn't leave her like that.

He went to close his eyes.

But just before he did...

"Oh, good. It looks like I made it in time."

...there came a lighthearted voice, completely out of place in this situation.

Everyone immediately looked up.

There, they saw a woman with gray hair.

* * *

"...Who are you?" asked Kou with a frown. He was looking at a woman with long gray hair wearing a robe of the same color. She looked like a magician from out of a fairy tale.

The whole group was wary, but the woman smiled gently at them. "It's all right now. You don't have to worry."

"Wait. Who are you?" asked Hikami. "You don't seem to be our enemy, at least..."

"Of course I'm not your enemy," she replied. "I'm more like a mother to all you cute little children." There was no hint of hostility or anger in her voice. In this situation, however, her words were anything but normal. Everyone was confused, and the air was thick with tension.

The woman paid all this no mind. She walked over, casual as could be, and sat down beside Tsubaki with a huff.

Mirei tensed, but the woman merely checked Tsubaki's wound with graceful movements. She reached into the bag she was carrying and took out a vial of medicine. Still speaking casually, she whispered, "My precious Green Princess, please heal this girl."

"Yes, Mother."

Out from behind the woman stepped a tiny figure. The beautiful green-haired little girl gave a nod.

Kou could tell she wasn't human. She was one of the Princess Series.

They were all taken aback as Green Princess stretched out her arms to touch Tsubaki's stomach. A gentle light enveloped the horrific injury, and little by little, she drew out the metal shard. The wound sealed as she did. No blood came out.

As the woman watched this impressive feat, she said in a sweet tone, "Green Princess is one of the Princess Series, specialized in recovery. She can even manipulate the structures of the human body. She's sealing the wound as the metal fragment leaves the organs... She can do that, you know. I'm also going to inject the girl with something, just to make sure she doesn't experience shock when she wakes up."

The woman smiled softly, like a doctor giving an explanation to her patient.

Eventually, the treatment was complete.

The woman lovingly stroked the little girl's green hair. Green Princess's face looked as content as a cat lying in a patch of sun, and she leaned into the woman's hand. The woman narrowed her gray eyes and nodded once, then turned to look at Kou and the others again.

"You don't have to be on guard with me. A little birdie told me there were some children skipping class to go into the ruins today. I was worried something might happen, so I came after you. I will do anything for Pandemonium... I received permission to come back here a week ago after I finished off a major surgery for the Empire. I'm happy to be able to work for the benefit of all my beloved children."

"...Could you be—?"

"Yes. I've been busy and had to delay my arrival, but...I am Pandemonium's third teacher."

The woman pressed a hand to her chest and told them her name with pride and dignity.

"I am Kurone Fukagami."

She was the third teacher of Pandemonium, one of the those previously sent to defend the empire.
She, too, had returned.

The Bride of Demise

7. THE KING OF THE KIHEI

【Memories from the Beginning of the End: Kagura】

Hmm, did I see this coming?

I mean, is there really even any point in asking that? Whether I saw it coming makes no difference now. He made his decision. And a lot of other kids went along for the ride. That's it. The only thing we can do now is watch over them, see them off.

And maybe…pray.

Yeah. Pray that everything goes well for them.

Not that I have anything to pray to. Haven't for a long time. It'd be nice if there was something. I really do wish there was.

Oh, but I can't help hoping anyway.

Hoping they'll be happy, that is.

* * *

"Ack, Kurone!"

Those were the first words out of Kagura's mouth when he saw

Kurone Fukagami. It seemed he wasn't aware she had returned. It also seemed he didn't particularly get along with her.

Kurone, on the other hand, offered him a motherly smile. She spread her arms and embraced him, rubbing her cheek against his. "I'm home, my dear little Kagura. Isn't it wonderful? No need to look so unhappy."

"Aaagh, stop it! That's so gross!" he cried. "I thought I told you before—I don't like that!"

"Oh, no need to be grumpy. My love is given equally to all."

"I don't want any of it!"

"Kagura, I have something more important to tell you!" cried Kou in a panic.

"More important?" asked Kagura.

Kou told him about what they had seen in the ruins. Kagura's expression quickly grew serious, and with utter calm, he whispered, "I see. So it's come to that."

Then Kagura was on the move—and fast.

He went to the ruins, confirmed the existence of the abnormal incubation nests, and destroyed them. Next, he submitted a survey request to the Department of Exploration. The students of that department then began their survey, with the requirement that they retreat and return alive if they discovered any more abnormal nests. They were focused primarily on the Clean Zones, and every nook and cranny was searched, including previously surveyed areas.

The results confirmed their worst fears.

They found that abnormal propagation was occurring in almost every ruin, though the scale varied from location to location. And that was only in the areas the students were able to search. It was too terrifying to even imagine the situation beyond.

Kagura's next move was to destroy all the newly discovered incubation nests, one by one. It would be a while before he finished, though, factoring in the time it took to move between each location. Plus, not all ruins were the same.

And so Kagura gave Pandemonium their orders.

"I'm sending you to the tenth basement level of the central labyrinth.

Full Humanoids and Special Types appear regularly—it's extremely dangerous."

"I want you to search there."

Kagura spoke the orders fluently, and the students of Pandemonium listened, a serious expression on each of their faces.

There was a good reason for this mission.

The central labyrinth was one of the largest ruins the Academy was aware of. Despite that, no abnormal incubation nests had been found within its Clean Zones. It was hard to believe the central labyrinth alone was free of nests, especially considering what they'd found in the others.

The issue was how far down the nests were located. Using other ruins of a similar size as reference, it was thought likely the abnormal incubation nests would be on the tenth basement level. But that location was too dangerous for the Department of Exploration to survey.

Considering the ruin's size, however, they couldn't just leave it alone.

And that was where Pandemonium came in.

"All twenty-three of you who survived the Gloaming will be going. Our aim is to find these abnormal incubation nests, and with a place this size, you'll need all the help you can get. Flowers and Wasps must travel in groups. If you encounter a Full Humanoid or a Special Type, retreat. The Phantoms will be supporting the others. When you find the nests, return to the Academy immediately."

Kagura asked if there were any questions, and one Wasp Rank girl casually raised a hand. In a light, seemingly careless tone, she asked, "You going to cry if we die?"

"I will. Of course I will," Kagura replied flatly. "No matter how many times I experience it, I'll never get used to someone in Pandemonium dying. But your current mission is nothing compared to the Gloaming. I know you can handle it. And though the higher-ups have stopped me from joining you this time, you won't be alone. Your third teacher and healing specialist, Kurone Fukagami, and your second teacher, Shuu Hibiya, will be going with you. No one should die so long as you keep on your toes."

"Okaaay," said the girl, lowering her hand.

Kou figured having the two teachers with them would greatly improve their combat power. And it was true this situation was significantly less dangerous than the Gloaming. But that didn't change the fact that it would be a fierce battle for the Flower and Wasp Ranks—and maybe even the Demon Ranks.

It's our duty as Phantom Ranks to make sure everyone makes it back alive. He knew that all too well. He clenched his hands into fists.

In the end, the search for Asagiri had been shelved for the time being.

He'd known the whole time. The moment she went missing in the ruins, there was no chance she would come back alive. It was just difficult to give up. He had to help her—after all, she'd protected him.

But Pandemonium had their duties. The only path forward was that which led to battle.

"All right. Destroy them—as many as your strength allows."

With that, Kagura declared the start of the mission.
Everyone in Pandemonium stood.
Then the whole class bowed.

* * *

The tenth basement level of the central labyrinth was a world of blue. Most of the ruin's walls were made of light-emitting material.

It was both beautiful and disconcerting to see everything dyed in blue. A human who spent too long down here might be driven insane, their mind eaten away through their retinas. It seemed entirely possible, so strange was this place.

"This...is the tenth level?"

"Is this your first time here, Kou?" asked Black Princess. "I've been here many times, but it is dangerous for humans. White Princess and I will protect you... But don't let your guard down."

"It's okay, Black Princess. I won't. We Phantoms have to be on guard at all times."

As they spoke, the sharp sound of heels striking the floor could be heard ahead of them. Shuu Hibiya led the group from the front. Kurone Fukagami held up the rear, smiling.

Without looking back at Kurone, Hibiya spoke in a clear tone. "Everyone here? We'll start our investigation of the central labyrinth now."

Beside them was a small girl. Hibiya didn't normally bring their Bride along, since they were already exceptionally skilled in combat, to the point that no one else's help was necessary. But this time, Pandemonium was going up against kihei, so it made sense to bring her along. The girl was a blue-haired beauty with a chilly attitude.

Kou had heard she was one of the Princess Series.

Hibiya called her name—or more likely, her alias.

"Nursery Rhyme and I, together with the Phantom Ranks, will be moving around to provide support, but it will take time to contact us. There will be many instances where we won't be able to react immediately. Protect yourselves. Never let your guard fall."

"Of course."

"We are Pandemonium."

"We will survive on our own strength."

Hibiya's words garnered several responses.

The members of Pandemonium bowed, then moved in their assigned directions. Most of the Flowers and Wasps were skilled at recovery or communications. Kou ran through the ruins, listening in on their reports.

In particular, Hikami's Unknown was doing exceptional work.

"There are no kihei down the eastern path as far as I can tell... The west and the south are dangerous. Kou, I can see something threatening at the rear of a group of three Flowers. Is that...a Special Type? Please confirm."

If you were judging by usefulness alone, Hikami's Bride's ability would surpass even a Demon Rank. Once Unknown split into pieces, Hikami was as good as a whole squad of scouts. Many people were moving based on his instructions.

Kou, too, was running after the group of three, as he'd been told. He caught sight of a Special Type, cloaked in a membrane, following the group from a distance. The membrane spread out behind it, like the wings of a mosquito.

"Hah!"

Kou threw his blade at it. Just as he pinned the Special Type against a wall, White Princess stepped forward.

"I'd ask you not to get in our way," she said, slashing once with her mechanical wings.

The kihei split vertically, and its complex internal mechanisms cascaded out. There was an explosion of synthetic blood, and the kihei convulsed, then stilled. With the three Flowers now safe, Kou went back to searching.

As he and the others fought, Kou learned the meaning behind Hibiya's Bride's alias, Nursery Rhyme.

Rather than a story, it's more like a lullaby.

Nursery Rhyme's weapon was sound waves. She destroyed kihei using sounds emitted on a special wavelength. The sound she created was very similar to the kind of tune you might sing to put a child to sleep. Incidentally, it seemed like she couldn't speak; she only knew how to sing.

Kurone Fukagami, on the other hand, was bouncing between students, a huge smile on her face.

"Hee-hee, everything will be all right! No matter what your injury is, your mother is here to put you back the way you were. Even if your head's lopped off, I can just pop it right back on, as long as we do it quickly!"

No matter how wounded a person was, Green Princess could fix them. Just having her and Kurone present would significantly lower their death rate. Kou was certain of that.

As Kou and the others continued to engage the enemy, a communication came in from a group of Flowers.

"We found them, the abnormal incubation nests! But—but that's—Agh!"

There was a disquieting cry, then the insect-shaped Bride's message cut out. Kou and the others who had received it hurried toward the Flowers' location, but there were still other requests for help from other Flowers.

As they stood unsure of what to do, Hibiya took Nursery Rhyme's hand and said, "I'll handle the other requests. All Phantom Ranks head to the nests."

Leaving the rest to Hibiya, Kou and the others rushed off.

Eventually, the Phantoms reached the specified location.

And there, they saw something impossible.

* * *

A pool of blood spread across the floor of the ruin. Vivid red had been splattered across the blue stone. Beside the pool lay the remains of two Flower Rank girls. Their skin had been flayed and their bodies opened up as though someone had neatly dissected them.

Not much time had passed since the transmission. This eerie sight shouldn't have been possible.

Before the lumps of flesh stood a person—a man with long white hair. His all-white clothes were soaked with a bright-red liquid.

The man looked dazed, like he didn't know what he'd done or even who he was. But there were chunks of flesh crammed beneath his nails and intestines wrapped around his fingers.

Why was there another human in the ruins?

Doubt filling his mind, Kou asked, "Did you...do this?"

Had this man killed Kou's companions? Had he turned them—the members of Pandemonium who'd managed to survive the Gloaming—into pitiful chunks of meat?

"Did you kill them?!"

"...Kou," said White Princess, "I don't think it matters how many times you ask him."

Yurie nodded in agreement as she rubbed her eyes. Shirai remained silent, his arms crossed. Sasanoe, too, said nothing, but he kept his sword at the ready.

The next person to speak was Black Princess. "That thing...is probably not human."

Suddenly, the man turned to look directly at Kou and the others.

His eyes had a mysterious red glow to them, like they were made of glass.

Black Princess spoke again. "It's...a kihei!"

"Ah, how long it has been," said the man. "The black princess, our former queen." Then he smiled and snapped his fingers.

Kou, White Princess, and Black Princess instantly disappeared from the room.

Their vision went white.

* * *

When they came to, they were inside an entirely white room. In the center was a twisted, long table made from warped stone, along with some chairs. The man was sitting in one of them, staring at Kou and the Princesses, an elegant smile still on his lips.

After a few seconds, Kou realized what had happened.

"Forced teleportation?"

Teleportation magic required extremely high skill. It was incredibly difficult for a human to accomplish it without the help of a magic device. That was especially the case when you were trying to teleport someone against their will. But this man had done it in an instant.

This was incredibly odd.

The Princesses stepped forward to protect Kou. As they did, the man calmly introduced himself.

"I am the new king of the kihei. Unfortunately, I don't yet have a name."

"...A kihei that can speak?" asked Kou.

"Is that really so surprising? Those of your Princess Series can speak, after all. It's absurd that you would be taken aback by something you've already seen demonstrated." The man shrugged. Despite what he was saying, the average kihei was not capable of communication, and Kou was shocked by this exception. The man gave an intelligent smile and said, "I do apologize for earlier. It's been so long since I've met a human. I just had to see what was inside."

"...You bastard."

"As a thank you for giving me the opportunity to see such *interesting* things, I'll let you know something about us." The man gracefully spread his arms and continued smoothly without waiting for a reply. "Up until now, the kihei have chosen whichever among them was strongest as their king or queen, without any specific intent. This

is because kihei, by their very nature, crave a leader. Now, after the Gloaming, their total numbers have grown, along with their shared desires. Spurred along by those desires, they created certain incubation nests—nests to create more soldiers—and even more special nests."

The man pointed to his chest. Drops of red trickled down his body.

Still covered in human blood from the top of his head to the tips of his fingers, he continued.

"They made an incubation nest in order to create me, a king who exists only for them. And so I was born. It was just after the former queen abandoned her duties, after all. So there was nothing to stand in the way of my birth." He stared at Black Princess as he spoke.

Kou fixed his eyes on this creature, this thing that called itself the king of the kihei but looked like a mere human. His appearance was extremely abnormal. He didn't have any of the usual characteristics of the kihei. There was a spot on his arm where it looked like something had eaten away at the flesh, but just like the Princess Series, his appearance was a complete imitation of a human's.

Just then, a particular memory replayed in Kou's mind.

There was a little girl walking, wearing a white hospital gown. She wasn't a kihei. She was just a human. Only her hair had been turned purple.

An adult was holding her hand, and she asked him:

"Everyone will love me when I'm the Opening Ceremony?"

The adult told her yes. He nodded, as if it was beyond question.
The girl laughed in excitement and smiled cutely.
She just wanted to help people.
She never thought her role would be to start a war.
The thought never even crossed her mind.
She had never imagined that she would be broken.
Hated by everyone.
That they would try to kill her again.

She just…

Wanted to be an ally of justice.

"The Princess Series...and you...no, all kihei—what are they?" asked Kou, forgetting his anger. He realized something as he spoke. This was a forbidden question, something that must never be asked.

But the man answered easily.

"Why do some kihei desire a human master? Why do so many crave and obey a king? Why do they kill humans without reason? The answer is simple. Just like the Princess Series, we are prehistoric weapons created to kill people."

For a moment, Kou felt relief. He had suspected as much. He knew the Princess Series had been created in the prehistoric period as weapons. He'd already considered the possibility that the same was true of the other kihei.

But that wasn't the end, the man continued, revealing something even more shocking.

"As the war dragged on, magic technology ran amok. And that... changed many of us into weapons, against our will. In fact, that is what happened to most creatures from the prehistoric period. Once, we were all just simple living creatures. And I, in particular..."

The man gave a benevolent smile.

And in an ever so gentle voice, he said:

"I was a human, just like you."

The Bride of Demise

8. THE REAL ENEMY

【Memories from the Beginning of the End: Helze】

Did I see this coming? Nope. Not one bit. But if Hibiya tells me to do it, then I'll just nod and go along. We'd just about reached our limits, anyway. Even a sad little puppet's got their problems, I guess. I just felt like the place we were back then wasn't going to work out much longer. So his offer was kind of like a lifeboat. I sorta liked the guy, too. Now I just have to let the tide take me where it will. That's what I was thinking when I agreed. I bet the others felt the same.

We don't make a habit of worrying about decisions we've already made... I doubt anyone's too upset.

But I get the feeling he's worrying about it secretly.
Still, I bet he'll keep moving forward. Hee-hee.

I kinda like that about him, you know?

* * *

"I suppose I should say all the kihei that dismembered themselves and put their parts into the incubation nest were originally human," said the man. "That would be more accurate. It is true that if you go back far enough, my origin is human. That is why my mind is as close to a human's as possible."

"Kihei were originally human?" repeated Kou, though he wasn't that surprised. He'd had an inkling of that, too. He had been nearly certain it was true of the Princess Series, at least, since the memory he'd glimpsed from the lost number five had belonged to a human.

"Will you continue to kill beings that used to be exactly the same as you?" asked the man.

"Of course," responded Kou without a moment's hesitation. This revelation made no difference to his decision. It didn't matter that the kihei were living creatures from the prehistoric period—or that those creatures included humans. They were now weapons in every regard. "So long as kihei continue to slaughter humans without reason, I will continue to stand against them."

"How unfortunate... That does put me in a difficult position." The man stroked his chin. He seemed genuinely troubled as he continued. "As we destroyed ourselves and were born anew, over and over again, the only thing we kihei held on to was our urge to destroy humans... Every once in a great while, a kihei would appear that regained their ability to think. Desiring someone to lead them, to save them from the loneliness and emptiness of their own existence, they became your Brides. Except for the Princess Series, true 'first generation' kihei, that have never been dismembered or propagated... All other kihei are unable to control their urge to kill. Even I, their king, am incapable of keeping them fully in check."

The man spoke fluently, then shook his head. Red droplets scattered around him. He didn't seem disgusted by the human blood in the least. That made it clear—though his words were gentle, this man was not humanity's ally.

White Princess stepped forward and asked, "Why did you bring us here?"

"Oh? I was simply curious about the former queen of the kihei and the man she serves. As the new king, I thought there might be something I could learn. I'm afraid it seems I will be disappointed, however." His words were ridiculous, but the man's actions didn't show any clear hostility.

Still, Kou remained wary. This man had killed his classmates, after all.

Seeing Kou's expression, the man looked taken aback. Then he shrugged and said, "I suppose it is my fault, even if I hadn't intended to do it. To make up for it, I will give you some good news."

"...Good news?"

"It's about the girl taking up half your mind at the moment... We didn't kill her. I know of a Type B that saw her. Um, yes, wait just a moment." The man put a finger to his forehead and closed his eyes.

Kou held his breath.

The man had been able to read Kou's thoughts, right down to the subconscious level. He figured that had something to do with the fact that most of his body was made of organic components modeled on those of the kihei. It seemed this man had access to other kihei's memories. Kou thought about the insane numbers of kihei residing in the ruins.

That would mean, when it came to what went on inside the ruins, this man was nearly omniscient.

Before long, he said, "...When the Type B attacked, the girl hid in the shadows inside the ruins and contacted someone. Then she, along with the human who came to her, disappeared. It wasn't a kihei that caused her to go missing. There have been a few other similar occurrences, though they are few."

"You mean there are multiple instances of humans causing people to go missing?" asked Kou.

"Exactly... You've said you will continue to stand against the kihei." The man stood. Drops of blood splattered to the floor. An arrogant smile spread across his face as he continued. "But can you really say, when all is said and done, that humans are your allies?"

The answer was obvious. Kou already knew.

Most humans...

...were not on their side.

* * *

"I do find your complexity fascinating," said the man. "Truthfully, I wish to observe you even more. I'd rather talk less about myself and hear more about you. Alas, we are nearly out of time. The new soldiers are worried about me, and they've gone on the move. A king does have his duties. I must return."

"Wait! I still have a lot of questions to ask you!" shouted Kou. This man had information on the kihei's perspective, information no one else had ever had. Kou couldn't let him get away.

Suddenly, the man gazed at Kou as if he were looking at a baby. White Princess and Black Princess leaped in front of their Groom and spread their wings wide.

They must have sensed a change in the man. White Princess whispered, "Kou, he's dangerous. He could kill you easily if he tried."

"But we won't let him," added Black Princess. "If he wants a fight, he can fight us."

"Come now, don't misunderstand. I was just thinking how cute he is. I have no desire to fight you, yet." The man raised his arms, and the tangle of intestines fell from his fingers. As if soothing a child, he said, "We shall meet again, little boy, as long as you stay out of harm's way. Then you and I must come to a decision."

"What decision?"

"If the ones to survive should be the kihei...

...Or the humans who betray you."

The man snapped his fingers, activating the forced teleportation magic. Kou and the Princesses were sent away from the white room.

At the same time, a roar filled their ears. The three of them opened their eyes to take in their new surroundings. And there, before them, was a metallic beast kihei formed from the bodies of countless Children.

* * *

"Ugh, what—?"

"Kou, I see you've made it back. Who was that man?" asked Sasanoe as he swung his sword, cutting off one of the Beast's front legs. It lost its balance, and its head careened forward as Crimson Princess fired off a round of liquid mercury bullets. The Beast fell, but the battle wasn't over.

There were over twenty of these Beasts in total.

Their current location was a particularly large room, even for the central labyrinth. Everyone was gathered there, fighting. It looked like Pandemonium had been attacked while Kou and the Princesses were gone, and everyone had gathered together to maximize their defense.

Kou quickly moved to Sasanoe's side. He took a feather from White

Princess and hacked a leg off a nearby Beast, following up with a vertical slash through the creature's open jaw.

Kou seamlessly joined the flow of battle as he spoke. "The man disappeared. I'll report the details later."

"Sounds good," replied Sasanoe. "Right now, we have these Beasts to deal with. They just keep coming."

There were a lot of them. Their defenses weren't as strong as the Baby's, so there was no need to remove their core parts, but they were faster. On top of that, they would try to self-destruct at regular intervals.

Right before they could do so, Yurie's Sister would strike their head, or Shirai's Nameless would crush their chest. Nursery Rhyme was also using the vibrations from her directional sound waves to break them apart. Even Hibiya was attacking, striking their joints with bare fists.

And yet there was no end in sight.

"I'll fight, too!" cried White Princess.

"…I will, as well," said Black Princess, and the two of them began blowing away the Beasts.

Each Beast went down faster than the last. However, Babies were joining the enemy's ranks. The addition of these new, highly defensive kihei plunged the battlefield into even further chaos. Both types were much more powerful than other kihei.

Kou began to panic. No matter how much fighting was necessary, the Phantom Ranks would likely get out alive. But outnumbered to this degree, the Flowers and Wasps were in danger.

Assessing the situation, he clenched his jaw. They weren't getting anywhere like this.

Black Princess suddenly approached him and whispered, "Kou… Kagura has forbidden me from using my true power. However, he will allow me to unleash it in one case only—when Pandemonium is in great danger and when every member can be protected… Right now, Sasanoe and the others are here, too. I can act. What I mean is: It's time for me to make my move." Black Princess closed her eyes for a moment, then opened them. She placed a hand on her ample bosom and said, "I want you and the other Phantom Ranks to protect everyone, so the aftershock of my attack won't harm them."

"Understood… But will you be okay pushing yourself?"

"I will be fine... I will finish this quickly." She gave Kou a fleeting smile.

He was about to tell her not to do it, but her eyes seemed to be asking him to have faith in her. He nodded. Then he called out, "Everyone switch to defense! Black Princess is going all out!"

"Millennium Black Princess?!" Sasanoe reacted a step quicker than the others. Once, in the past, he'd traded blows with her directly. Now he ordered everyone to form a circle. If anyone moved too slowly, Hibiya grabbed them by the collar and pulled them along. The last one to leap into the circle was Kurone, still smiling. Shirai's Nameless covered them all.

Black Princess was the only one outside the circle. She slowly reached her arms forward. Before the Babies and the Beasts stood the former queen of the kihei, her wings spread.

Black feathers fell like snow.

"It's time to rest, soldiers who know nothing but battle. I wish you pleasant dreams."

Black feathers froze in midair. Out of the darkness formed a black sphere, which morphed into a cube and exploded all at once in a flurry of needles.

Soundlessly, the needles pierced through the Babies and Beasts. Those that passed near Pandemonium were shattered by Hibiya, Yurie, and Sasanoe.

The queen's rampage was silent and overwhelming. Everything died and was destroyed.

Black Princess watched it all with a sorrowful gaze.

Eventually, Kou and the others could no longer see anything moving. Black Princess turned back to them and released a heavy breath. She bowed gracefully despite her unsteady feet.

And so their duty was complete.

Leaving them with mountains of new, unsettling information.

9. ISUMI'S TEARS

【Memories from the Beginning of the End: Hibiya】

Did I predict this outcome?
What purpose does that question serve? It's already decided.
There's no point in asking about it. They chose. They decided. We adults shouldn't meddle. They have a future. They have the right to live. That's all there is to it.
If you want to laugh, then laugh. I'll snap your neck in a second.
I will not allow anyone to look down on them for their decision.

All that is expected of us is to see them off.

* * *

Kou Kaguro was lying on the couch in his room with his eyes closed. He was reflecting on the battle from the other day.
That, and his own ruthlessness.
Two of his classmates had been sacrificed in the cruelest of ways. He hadn't interacted much with those two girls, but he knew their names—Mitsuba and Matsuri.
Despite their deaths, Kou hadn't gone back in time.
That fact weighed on him, but the situation was still in chaos.
The kihei's abnormal propagation... Their new soldiers... Their king.
Kou had reported the information he had on the king to Hibiya the

moment the battle ended. He reported what the king had told him as well, but only the parts he thought it would be all right for Sasanoe and the others to hear.

If the teachers deemed it necessary, they could tell the rest of the students about the kihei's true nature.

Kou had received mountains of valuable information. He had no idea how things would turn out, but there was one fact that had taken root in his mind.

Asagiri disappeared because a human took her.

It was still a mystery why. He didn't even know where she'd disappeared to—or who had taken her. He racked his brain, but no answers came.

As he thought, the face of a friend bubbled up in his mind.

Now that I think about it, I wonder how Isumi's doing.

Kou hadn't been able to meet up with him since Isumi had informed him Asagiri was missing. He'd been busy with the search and his Pandemonium duties. Now Kou was worried about him. Deep down, Isumi had a kind heart. And even if he didn't, he would be devastated by the disappearance of someone he loved.

Kou didn't know how the situation with the king of the kihei would unfold. If they were given an order to start a long-term war against him, then Kou might not have another chance to see his friend.

He sat up. Black Princess was lying on the bed, sleeping. It seemed she was still tired out. White Princess was beside her, her eyes closed. Seeing the two of them, black and white sleeping side by side, was like looking at a work of art.

Kou carefully stood up from the couch, trying not to wake them. Silently, he cut across the room. They were kihei; if they were on guard, they would wake up immediately. Thankfully, they were just relaxing.

Kou hurried out of the room, leaving his Brides asleep on the bed.

* * *

Kou had rushed out to see Isumi, but when he stopped to think, he realized he couldn't visit him in the Research dorms. He wasn't sure what to do.

However, in the end, he was able to find him with unexpected ease.

Kou overheard some students gossiping as they crossed the campus. They mentioned a strange male student in the communal cemetery.

Kou broke into a run. He had a bad feeling in the pit of his stomach.

As he ran, the sky above him was thick with clouds that seemed about to burst. He rushed up the street, his feet pounding the pavement. The air was heavy and humid as he left the shops and Academy buildings behind.

Finally, he found Isumi.

"Isumi…"

"Hey…Kou…"

There was a large garden on the far side of the hill that housed the graves of people whose death was not attributed to the Gloaming. Fist-size gravestones poked up from between the flowers with nothing but simple names engraved on them.

Isumi was standing in front of Kou Kaguro's grave.

Below the gloomy sky, he looked up at Kou in a daze. His hands were bound in glove-like restraints. Kou's breath caught at the strange sight. Isumi looked at Kou with puffy reddened eyes and raised a hand in greeting. As he did so, his gaze landed on the restraints binding him.

He gave a troubled laugh. "Oh, this… They finally stuck these on me after I tried over and over to put on magic armor and go out looking for Asagiri. They won't take them off unless someone's watching me at all times. Makes it impossible to go about my normal life… Pretty crappy situation, don't you think?"

"…Isumi, are you really—?"

"Hey, Kou… You're alive, yeah? Asagiri's got to be alive, too, right?" Isumi smiled, his gaze hollow.

Finally, Kou realized why Isumi was in front of his grave. The only thing Isumi could do right now was pray. He must come here all the time to do just that, visiting Kou's grave to pray that Asagiri returns just as miraculously.

Isumi's face twisted like he was about to burst into tears. His eyes looked so innocent as words began to fall from his mouth. "I…had a sister."

"Huh?"

"A sister, a little sister." Out of nowhere, Isumi began speaking about his past. His eyes were vacant, and his words fell like unsteady drops of rain. "She'd call after me, follow me wherever I went. She was so cute. But she was killed by a kihei, along with my mom and dad, too. The wall in the slums where we lived broke. An arm like an insect's cut her head off. I watched it roll across the ground. I must have looked like an idiot with my mouth just hanging open."

Isumi gave a dry laugh. Kou was worried he was about to break, but he seemed surprisingly collected as he shook his head. Then he said something Kou hadn't expected.

"That's why... I'm sorry. I was jealous of you. Your family wasn't killed by the kihei; no one you knew was. I kept lashing out at you over and over... Even though your parents were killed, too, just by other humans."

"Isumi, it's all right. Don't worry about it... It doesn't really bother—"

"I'm sorry... I'm so sorry. It's because I'm like this... That's why Asagiri's gone, isn't it? It's because I only do bad things. It's my punishment."

"Isumi..."

Isumi fell to his knees like his body was crumbling, and large tears welled in his eyes. Kou rushed over to him and placed a hand on his shaking shoulder in an attempt to console him.

Tears spilled down Isumi's cheeks as he continued to confess. "I did the same thing back then, when you distracted the kihei. I'd decided I was going to protect Asagiri, but I just made you do everything. I forced it all on you and ran... It's because I'm like this... That's why!"

"Isumi, you didn't do anything wrong!" Kou shouted. "You don't have anything to do with Asagiri going missing!" But Isumi wasn't listening.

He continued, his eyes vacant. "It's my fault... I'm sorry, I'm sorry, oh God... Please bring her back. Please bring Asagiri back... I couldn't save her... I couldn't protect her—"

"Isumi!"

Kou's shout was like a slap in the face. He looked into Isumi's eyes.

Isumi's gaze wandered, like he was dazed, but his focus eventually settled on Kou. Kou gave a slight nod. He couldn't tell Isumi the details yet, but he put everything he had into his next sentence.

"It's okay, Isumi. Asagiri is alive."

Asagiri had gone with another person of her own volition and disappeared. It was unlikely she'd suddenly died after that.

There was still hope.

"I am certain Asagiri is still alive," said Kou.

Isumi stared at him. After a moment, he smiled. "Yeah, you're right… She must be."

He squeezed Kou's hand, the one on his shoulder, clutching at it desperately.

In a murmur resembling a prayer, he said, "Thank you, Kou… And uh…"

"What is it?"

"Will you be my friend?" Isumi asked timidly.

Kou gave him a questioning smile, then a firm nod and said, "We've been friends for a long time."

Isumi kept saying thank you, over and over and over again.

Eventually, rain began to fall, but even then Isumi didn't try to stand. Pulling him up, Kou dragged him from the communal cemetery. He chose a path that would protect Isumi from the rain as much as possible and returned him to the dorm.

He had to find Asagiri, for Isumi's sake, too.

His resolve had grown even stronger.

* * *

"Kooou!"

"…Kou."

As soon as Kou opened the door, his Brides came flying at him. They were supposed to be sleeping side by side. Before he could even feel surprise, however, the two were wrapped around him.

They squeezed him tightly, the soft curves of their bodies pressing against him.

The impact nearly sent him sprawling to the floor, but he managed to remain standing. He shuffled into the room with the black and white masses still attached to him. Eventually, he managed to get over to the bed and sit down.

"What's wrong, you two?" he asked.

"We woke up, and you weren't here."

"Did you go somewhere again?"

"Sorry I didn't say anything before leaving. I went to see Isumi."

"To see Isumi…"

Neither of the Princesses had met Isumi in person, but they'd heard about him from Kou. They sat up straight on the bed when they heard his name, neatly folding their legs.

"That's the boy who was close to Asagiri, right?" said White Princess.

"Is he all right?" asked Black Princess. "It's been quite some time since she went missing…"

Kou shook his head in response. He thought of Isumi in the rain and said, "He's really worn down. I have to bring Asagiri back for his sake, too, but…"

"I wonder who took her?" said White Princess. Kou nodded.

Ultimately, they couldn't do anything until they figured that out.

Kou bit his lip. He wove his fingers together and stared into the distance. Then hands touched his hair. His Brides stroked his head—White Princess gently and Black Princess awkwardly.

Kou cocked his head in confusion and asked, "What's up?"

"We don't want you to worry too much. Asagiri and Isumi are your friends; we understand how you feel. You're concerned. It's painful. Which is why…"

"…We don't want you to run yourself down. You are important to us."

After saying that, the two hugged him again. Their soft white and black hair caressed his neck. They were warm, even though they were kihei. Kou felt the gentle heat from their bodies relaxing him.

He put one arm around each of them, hugged them back, and thought, *If I didn't have these two…my heart would be in pieces, just like Isumi's.*

Kou recalled when Kagura had used the term *operation limit*. His body was nearing its limit, but his mind should have crumbled long ago. His two Brides were a huge reason why it hadn't.

"It's okay, you two," he said. "I won't break, and I'll bring Asagiri back. I'll look into the other instances the king mentio—"

Just then, he realized he'd overlooked something. These other

instances the kihei mentioned—when exactly had they started? Had
they stopped?

"...It can't be."

"Kou?"

"...Kou?"

"Sorry, I have to go out... Don't worry, though!" He sprang up and
rushed immediately out the door.

There was a chance he'd overlooked an important possibility.

* * *

A lot of people went missing from the Academy, and every incident was
summarized and recorded. They were even publicly available as part of
the Academy's combat records.

Kou ran to the library. He hurried between the heavy wooden bookshelves without making a sound. He went to a shelf deep in the library
where there weren't many students and pulled out the substantial list of
missing people.

He didn't see any patterns in the rows of records. But as he checked
the list, he paid attention to one thing in particular.

*"A week ago, some students went missing while the Department of Com-
bat was in the middle of making a Clean Zone. The whereabouts of the
two girls are still unknown. Five days ago, a girl from the Department of
Exploration went missing. Two days ago, another girl went missing from
the same department. And now, Asagiri Yuuki."*

Finally, Kou could see it. About the same number of female students were disappearing in a similar fashion at regular intervals. Kou
clenched his fists.

This may not be the first time all this has happened, he thought, just as
something unexpectedly hit his shoulder. He whirled around.

His eyes met a head of familiar white hair, and he blinked several
times.

It was Kagura.

"Kagura... This—"

"Yep. Looks like female students are being regularly kidnapped. Let's
go to the classroom." Kou did as Kagura asked.

They left the library, walked down the halls of Central Headquarters, and arrived at the classroom. Today's classes had already finished, so there was no one there.

Kagura and Kou stood facing each other in the empty classroom, just like always.

Kagura's tone was grave. "A handful of girls go missing on a regular basis. That makes me think they're being used for something. And the most likely use would be as…human test subjects."

"What?" Kou narrowed his eyes at the unsettling words. It was a possibility he didn't want to consider, one that brought back memories of the torturous modifications he'd endured as a child. Asagiri's innocent smile appeared in his mind, then slowly faded away.

Kagura shrugged. "I told you, didn't I? Said I'd look into Pandemonium and the higher-ups. I found a lead. Which is why I have a suggestion." He casually held up a finger and waved it from side to side. In a singsong voice, he continued:

"Let's go to the capital together."

That should have been impossible for a student.

And for Kou, it would mean finally overcoming one of his biggest obstacles.

The Bride of Demise

10. AT THE CAPITAL

【Memories from the Beginning of the End: Shirai】

Of course I didn't expect it to come to this.

But I don't have much to say about it.

I don't support them. I don't agree with them. I won't praise them.
But I don't want to slander them, criticize them, or blame them,
either.

They made that choice in order to live.

I can only pray their path is safe.

Even if that means they part ways with us.

* * *

There was a reason Kou Kaguro was able to visit the capital.
And it was directly related to Kagura's "lead."
"Your parents were at the forefront of human experimentation and
kihei research," explained Kagura. "Clearly, there had to be someone
powerful supporting them from behind the scenes. But they were discovered by regular soldiers and executed on the spot. You were reported

as a victim of their experiments, and this patron of theirs couldn't move to take you with their opponents and the public watching. On top of that, you'd lost all memories to do with your parents, and on the surface, you don't appear to have had any major modifications made. So they decided you weren't of significant value and sent you off to the Academy… And that's where I thought I'd do a little digging."

Kagura explained all this as they walked down the hallway in Central Headquarters. The hard click of his shoes and the smooth sound of his voice reverberated down the hall before eventually fading. What had Kagura done? Kou got an ominous feeling and frowned.

Kagura continued confidently, with no sign of remorse. "You regained your memories of your parents, and I let that information leak. I've always had the right to take one student with me when I go to the capital, but they were pretty firm about refusing to let me bring you, since you're a bit of a wild card… But this time, they specifically invited you."

"Who invited me?"

"A bigwig medical researcher in the capital," Kagura replied leisurely. "He wants to ask about your parents. I doubt he'll suddenly try to dissect you, but you should hide as much about yourself as you can."

Kou understood. In other words, Kagura had used him as bait. He didn't love the idea, but Kou was ready for the challenge. This was a small price to pay if it meant finding a clue to Asagiri's whereabouts.

Kagura suddenly stopped walking and turned to Kou. Kou was trying to determine what was wrong when Kagura muttered, "…I think it's about time for them to summon us."

As he spoke, there was a change in their bodies. A blue light shimmered around their skin, like they were encased in lightning, though there was no heat or shock.

Forced teleportation.

Just as Kou realized what was happening, his vision went white. The next moment, he was in a massive hall decorated primarily in vermilion. There was a space in the center surrounded by a fence, where a crystal the size of a large beast was enshrined. A complex magic circle was carved into the floor in front of it.

Kou only needed a glance to know what it was—the teleportation device linked to the capital rumored to be in Central Headquarters.

As the realization hit him, he gritted his teeth. *No one can enter this room unless they're teleported here by the operator inside.*

No matter how often he went back in time, Kou could never make it to this place on his own. It was an unsurmountable obstacle to him. The truth was: He had no way to get to the capital on his own.

As Kou fell into thought, a woman wearing a monocle approached and asked, "Kagura, are you ready?" She appeared to be the Central Headquarters employee in charge of the teleportation device. She looked like a simple office worker, but Kou knew what she really was— an advanced magic user.

"It is time to teleport," she announced in an emotionless, flat voice. "Have you made your preparations?"

"Yep. Ready when you are," replied Kagura casually, and Kou nodded in agreement.

Even if I wanted to bring my Brides along, I wouldn't be allowed to.

The woman led Kagura to stand in front of the crystal. The magic circle glowed blue throughout the whole process. Kou stepped into the circle as well and felt a tingling along his skin like static electricity.

The woman with the monocle made a slow, gentle motion with her hands, and a panel appeared in midair. As she tapped at it, she said, "You are now heading to the capital, the place we must protect. Have a pleasant journey."

A blinding light rushed across the crystal, then poured out with such force it was as if the sun itself had appeared before them.

Everything vanished from Kou's and Kagura's sight.

And so Kou leaped to a place he should never have been able to go.
A distant place, for which the Academy acted as a bulwark.
The imperial capital.

* * *

The scenery around them changed.

The next moment, Kou realized they were standing somewhere very strange.

"…This is…" He looked around. They were in a building far older-looking than he'd expected. The entrance hall was generously decorated with antique metal and real wood. Everything was steeped in the calm of polished wood and the solemnity of brass. Central Headquarters may have appeared fancier at a first glance with its decorations making use of magical technology, but all this must have cost considerably more.

Windows extended to either side, and Kou cast his gaze through those, as well. Outside was a smooth expanse of grass. Beyond it, a sailboat floated gracefully down a narrow river. Seeing this, Kou frowned. This was his first time seeing a boat, and that was no merchant ship, either. It was probably a personal vessel meant for enjoying the water, all without any fear of a kihei attack. Kou had a hard time believing it was possible to live such a carefree life.

Through the windows on the opposite side, he saw a beautiful forest dotted with villas. A questioning look appeared on Kou's face as he wondered where in the world they'd jumped to.

Kagura whispered, "This is the private residence of the doctor who invited us. We have permission to stay for one hour. We'll be forcefully teleported out when our time is up, and we won't be able to escape from here into the capital proper. Make sure you have the conversation you want to have—and quickly."

As he spoke, a man in servant attire appeared in front of them. This, too, was the sort of thing Kou had only heard about in stories. The man gave a deep bow to both of them, then addressed Kagura. "It has been some time, sir. I have heard of your accomplishments."

"Yeah, really has been a while, huh? The Academy's remained stable thanks to you all."

The two of them exchanged greetings, touching upon the Academy's status and the higher-ups. Then the servant looked over at Kou. He seemed to accept what he saw and shot a glance at Kagura, who nodded back.

"Apologies for the wait," the servant continued. "This way please, Master Kou Kaguro."

The servant motioned for Kou, and only Kou, to follow. Kagura stayed put as the servant walked off, Kou trailing behind.

As they traversed a hallway with an especially high ceiling, things like the bones of turtles and sharks—creatures Kou had only ever seen in books—decorated the space above their heads. For Kou, who had spent the majority of his life at the Academy, everything he saw here defied belief.

Eventually, the servant stopped. In front of them stood a heavy door made from a single piece of wood. The servant lifted the door knocker, held in the mouth of a lion, and gave it several raps.

A low, smooth voice reminiscent of aged wine called back. "Is it him?"

"Yes, he is with me."

"You may enter."

The servant opened the door, and Kou stepped in alone at his urging.

In contrast to the old-fashioned hallway, this room's interior was brimming with magic devices. There were countless magic crystals, glowing vials of medicine, kihei parts, and complex machines of unknown origin. Heavy research books lined the bookcases, and there was a whole Type B kihei suspended from the ceiling.

The door slowly closed behind him, and Kou faced the person inside the room. It was a man with lots of white hair and chestnut-colored eyes, dressed in luxurious clothing. He spoke softly. "My name is Kashmar Low. I am one of those supporting the Academy."

There, he stopped. Kou surmised the man didn't mean financial support alone. Most likely, he was an important person in the capital, too. But the man didn't try to explain anything in detail. It seemed he didn't intend to elaborate for the benefit of a mere student who did nothing but fight.

"So you're the asset the Kaguros left behind, I take it?" he asked imperiously.

Instantly, Kou knew this man did not see him as a person. If Kou gave the wrong reply, he might find himself back on the operating table, mere material for more experiments.

* * *

If he made a mistake, it would all be over.

With that in mind, he decided to start out by playing it safe.

"...I don't know if I should be called an asset or not. In the end, I'm just a failed experiment. My parents said they weren't able to make as many modifications as they'd hoped—that unfortunately, I wasn't suitable."

"Oh, really? Well, that's fine. I'm happy just to hear you remember that much. You lost everything the moment those damned soldiers shot the Kaguros... Do you recall anything else about your parents?" Kashmar's eyes narrowed as he asked.

As he took in the man's snakelike expression, Kou realized something. This was a test. In that case, he'd accept the challenge. He pressed his palm to his chest.

"There are several things I'm sure you'll be happy to hear," he said, choosing his words carefully. He started to share small pieces of information—his parents' interest in the Princess Series, their ideal of ending the war, and—omitting his own modifications—several experiments they had conducted with that goal in mind.

Lounging on a leather couch, Kashmar listened. He nodded several times. Eventually, he clapped his hands together, seeming impressed. "Wonderful. You were only ten years old when your parents died... Yet you remember so much. You speak without superfluous tangents—and precisely select and organize information to draw my interest. You have the same genius as your parents."

Kashmar's interest was now directed at Kou himself. Not wanting to pass up this opportunity, Kou began to reel him in.

"At the risk of sounding immodest, I've always thought the same myself. I have an interest in—a passion for my parents' research, and I have strived to maintain my studies... One day, I would like to walk the same path they did."

"Oh...?" Kashmar's eyes shone. He stroked his chin, clearly interested.

Got him. Kou narrowed his eyes. There had to be a lot of opposition to the field Kashmar supported. He would always be in need of more people he could trust, assistants in particular. The son of the Kaguros—former leaders in their field—would make a perfect candidate.

Kou made his next move. "Could I ask you something? My parents were constantly saying that we should learn more about the kihei... Did their line of research end with their deaths? Or are there still like-minded people working tirelessly to keep it alive?"

"You may rest assured, though I must not say anything too loudly," he said, lowering his voice. He stared at Kou. Kou gazed solemnly back. As if reading something into Kou's violet eyes, the man decided to continue. "The Kaguros' ideals live on. Experiments continue, even as we speak.... But regrettably, the majority no longer seek to end the war. Instead, they are attempting something very different."

Kou tensed. If Kashmar wasn't looking, he would have squeezed his fists. This essentially confirmed that kihei-related human experimentation were still taking place. Now all he needed to do was draw out as much information as possible.

Suppressing his excitement, Kou forced a saddened expression onto his face. Assuming an uneasy tone, he asked, "Something different?"

"They are working on new soldiers to combat the kihei. Experiments are taking place both here in the capital and at the Academy... The ones at the Academy are completely separate from my own. I don't even know who all is involved, let alone the details of their research... Eventually, I intend to dig deeper into their side of things."

In some ways, that was enough information for Kou. Both the Academy and the capital had the necessary materials for these experiments:

One had students, the other had orphans.

Students had plenty of magic, and no one would question them going missing. And the capital, for its part, had enough orphans to spare. Both sources had their merits. And that meant Asagiri and the other kidnapped girls had most likely been chosen as subjects for the Academy's experiments.

Just to be sure, Kou sought confirmation. "Is there any way I could participate in that research? I'd like to adjust its direction to pick up where my parents left off, carrying on their ideals. If possible, I'd like to guide the experiments."

"Well, you will have to give it some time. I admire your ambition, I really do, but it's too soon for that... And that's right; your Bride is a Princess Series, correct? You already have an excellent test subject at your disposal...Kou Kaguro."

Kashmar licked his lips and stood. Kou felt extraordinarily disgusted by the fact that Kashmar saw his Bride as a potential test subject. But he swallowed back his emotions and stood his ground.

Kashmar seemed impressed as he shook Kou's hand. "Why don't we consider this: Once you graduate, come work for me as an assistant. I am delighted to see the Kaguros' asset grown into such an excellent young man...truly delighted." Kashmar seemed to relish the thought as he spoke.

Internally, Kou felt like sticking out his tongue. Talking about his parents' experiments made him want to vomit. But he'd gained something here, and he'd managed to get it without Kashmar learning about his abilities or the modifications to his body. Plus, Kashmar's trust would be useful in the future.

If he does as he said and digs deeper into the experiments happening at the Academy...

Then there was a good chance Kou could learn something about Asagiri.

Just then, it seemed their time had run out. Somewhere, a clock chimed. Kashmar slipped a hand into his breast pocket and pulled out a gold pocket watch. Blue light sparkled around Kou.

With friendliness in his voice, Kashmar said, "I'll send for you again. Next time, I'll show you around the capital. Look forward to it."

"We'll meet again."

As Kou heard this final promise, his vision winked out.

With that, Kou's short visit came to an end, and he was returned to the confines of the Academy.

11. THE TIME THAT WON'T BE

【Memories from the Beginning of the End: Yurie】

I sooo did not see this coming. Not in my wildest dreams. Sister said the same thing. It's so sad, so lonely. But I don't think it's something bad.

Sister and I are going to keep doing our thing as Phantom Ranks. I won't think about anything that comes after. The kids who want to go can go. Just keep on walking; don't look back.

As for me, well…

I love all of them.

Even if they abandoned a lot of other people.

I still love them all!

* * *

Thanks to Kagura, Kou was able to learn several things. Research on the kihei involving human experiments was taking place even in the Academy. It was likely Asagiri and the other girls were chosen as test subjects for those experiments.

But that was as far as Kou had gotten. It would be difficult to learn anything more, but he now had a valuable source of information:

Kashmar.

If Kashmar looked into the experiments being conducted at the Academy, Kou could gain access to that information himself. If Kou became Kashmar's assistant, it might even broaden his ability to investigate on his own.

But that would take time.

After a serious discussion with Kagura, Kou made his decision.

He needed to be ready to dedicate over a decade of his life to this mission.

He would gain Kashmar's trust, build his status within the capital, and uncover the truth about the human experiments. Once he'd accomplished that, he would jump all the way back in time. Then he would take Asagiri back before she could fall into their clutches.

If possible, he would stop all human experimentation.

That was what he'd decided.

The problem was that Kou couldn't anticipate what the king of the kihei would do during that time. If a battle forced Kou to go back in time, he would have no other choice. He would have to go much farther back, monitor Asagiri, and keep her safe. It wasn't certain to work, but it had the advantage of placing less stress on Kou.

Regardless of what happened, he understood his mission.

He would take Asagiri Yuuki back. For her sake, for Isumi's sake, and for his own sake.

At this, Kagura offered him a thin smile. "I have to admire your determination, but this is the Academy. Even students in Pandemonium can die at any moment. In a way, deciding to protect a single girl at all costs is pretty stupid."

There was truth to what he said.

But Asagiri was Kou's friend. She had protected him. And the sound of Isumi's tearful apologies still lingered in Kou's ears.

Kou had no intention of giving up.

But he would learn something else, too. He was going to live for over a decade, knowing all the while that everything he experienced would be undone.

Kou would have to learn just how terribly hollow that felt.

* * *

On the battlefront, Kou's days searching for and destroying the abnormal incubation nests continued. He regularly fought against Babies and Beasts. But even running into powerful enemies and destroying them became routine.

The days and months flew by.

And as they did, Kou and his friends constructed a temporary peace.

"Kou, what do you think?"

He was in his dorm room in Central Headquarters. White Princess turned to face him, wearing a silvery-white dress that clung to her frame. There was a large, adorable ribbon on the back. This outfit was a little different from her regular, cute clothing—it had a mature elegance to it, as well. Her hair was done up in the same style Tsubaki had used some time ago.

She brought a hand to the low neckline of her dress and spun around. "How is it? You often tell me I'm beautiful, Kou, and it's not that I doubt what you say, it's just…I'm not sure. Do I look odd in this dress?"

"I think it looks wonderful on you, White Princess. You're very beautiful."

"Mm, I agree, White Princess. It suits you. But…is my dress all right?" Black Princess hesitantly joined the conversation.

She, too, wore a dress that clung to her figure. She spun around, showing the cute bow affixed to the back. Her dress, however, used much more fabric than White Princess's. It was a design that showed off very little skin—the exact opposite of how she looked as the queen of the kihei. Her hands, wrapped in silk gloves, moved gracefully and pressed against the flowers decorating her bosom.

Her hair was done up the same way as White Princess's.

"Yours is nice, too, Black Princess," Kou answered gently. "You both look wonderful."

*   *   *

Winter had already arrived.

Snow was piled high outside the buildings.

On this day, a party would be held to mark the end of one year and the beginning of another. Obviously, the students of Pandemonium couldn't celebrate with the regular students. Instead, Kagura forced the Academy to let them organize one of their own. It was to be a dance held in a large room in Central Headquarters.

Kou and the Princesses had just finished their preparations.

"Okay then, let's go, Kou. Take my hand."

"It's time to head to the dance, Kou. Take my hand."

The two of them held their delicate hands out to him. He politely accepted them.

Then, smiling, he made his way to the dance.

* * *

"Ah, they're here," said Tsubaki. "You're late. Your dresses are beautiful, though."

"They suit both of you perfectly," added Mirei. "And you look so different with your hair up."

The two girls, one short, one tall, were dressed up as well and looked gorgeous. Tsubaki was cute—her outfit all white with lots of ribbons and bows—while Mirei cut a more sensual figure in a simple dress of bright-red fabric. Her dazzling, pale décolletage peeked out from the dress's plunging neckline.

Hikami was watching her, a serious expression on his face and his arms crossed. "Mirei, don't you think you're showing a bit too much skin? As a student, shouldn't you be a little more, uh, modest?"

"Honestly, Hikami," said Yaguruma, "you can be a real pain sometimes."

"And why exactly am I a pain, Yaguruma?!" Hikami cried, baffled.

Yaguruma looked at the ceiling as if to say "Oh, I don't know…"

The two of them were wearing their military uniforms, as usual, along with their cloaks reserved for formal occasions. Kou was dressed the same. The boys were told they could dress how they pleased as well, but there weren't many who wanted to dress up.

The dance included a buffet.

No Brides were allowed at the party, aside from the Princess Series, out of concern that they would damage the facility. Despite their resulting disappointment, the twenty-one members of Pandemonium still made themselves at home under the light of the magic crystal lamps. Tsubaki already had a huge mound of food on her plate.

"Whoever manages to eat the most is the winner at these kinds of parties," she said.

"Hmm, did you forget about the dancing part?" asked Yaguruma. The two of them chattered excitedly.

Hikami sighed, a drink in one hand. "We still haven't learned anything new about the king of the kihei. Battles with the Babies and Beasts happen sporadically... But the whole thing is still shrouded in mystery and uncertainty. Should we really be enjoying ourselves like this?"

"It's fine, Hikami," replied Mirei. "We lie in the dark. But we should also be enjoying our lives at the Academy. This is part of our duties, too." She smiled and held out her glass.

After a moment of frowning and thinking, Hikami tilted his own glass. The two clinked their drinks together and smiled.

"Would you like to join me for a dance later?" asked Hikami.

"I'd love to."

Hikami took her hand and pulled her away from the group, the two of them engrossed in their own conversation.

Tsubaki turned away, looking enraged. "Why are they not a thing yet?" she muttered.

"My thoughts exactly." Yaguruma nodded emphatically.

But apparently, Hikami and Mirei were just friends, and that seemed like it would be the end of it.

Yaguruma followed Tsubaki's example and started piling his plate with food, followed by White Princess doing the same. She filled up a plate for Black Princess, too, adding everything she felt looked especially delicious. Black Princess took the plate with unsteady hands, clearly overwhelmed.

Kou watched them with a smile. Retreating from the hustle and bustle, he moved over to a window. Outside, the snow was falling silently. Each of the Academy buildings was covered in a thick blanket of white.

As he gazed out the window, he thought, *Asagiri... Isumi... I wonder how they're doing.*

It was difficult to say for certain that Asagiri was still alive. Too much time had passed. Kou had heard that Isumi's sanity was in tatters. He'd been sent to the Department of Medicine. Kou hadn't been able to see him since. He bit his lip, even though he knew he would be going back in time.

On the other hand, his interactions with Kashmar had progressed well.

And in the meantime, Kou had drawn up a list of all the people who had gone missing. He'd scrutinized every detail, hoping to find some commonalities among the circumstances of their disappearances. But everything was still too uncertain.

He was swirling his glass of sparkling water in his hand when he heard someone speak to him.

"I hear you've been going to see Kashmar. That does worry your mother."

He turned around and saw Kurone Fukagami.

* * *

Green Princess was practically stuck to Kurone's back, hiding. Kurone was wearing an emerald green dress that matched her Bride. She smiled, then took Kou's now-empty glass and placed it on a nearby table.

Gently, she said, "Kashmar was the first person to receive official permission to conduct research on the kihei, but there are rumors he is a Coexister. It would be dangerous to get too close to him. In the end, kihei are just weapons."

"...Thank you for the warning. But..."

"But what?"

"Is your own Bride just a weapon, too?" Kou asked. Her statement had been strange for a Groom.

Kurone nodded in understanding. She stroked Green Princess's hair as if she were doting on her own daughter. "This girl is different. She is a

Princess Series specialized in healing. She's my assistant. Or…rather, I'm her assistant. Either way, she is my precious partner." Her tone was gentle.

Kou nodded in acknowledgement.

Kurone turned back to Kou, her expression still kind. Then she warned him again. "Weapons only have meaning if they're used appropriately. The Coexisters' ideology is dangerous."

She bade him not to forget her words and walked away, her dress swirling behind her. Green Princess followed.

Kou thought about what Kurone had said. It was possible those who opposed the Coexisters had started seeing Kou as an enemy. He needed to be ready for the possibility that someone, perhaps the Puppets, would come to assassinate him.

He sighed, seeing even more headaches in his future. But just then, he heard her.

"Kou, let's dance."

Someone gently took his hand.

It was White Princess. She drew him toward the center of the room.

* * *

This wasn't the first time he'd danced with White Princess, if you counted all the times he'd undone.

He looked around him, moving his feet in time with the music. White Princess expertly twirled her dress. They danced together gracefully, smoothly.

Kou glanced over to see Black Princess staring at the two of them from afar. White Princess whispered in his ear.

"Black Princess asked me to do this. You seem very troubled lately, Kou. She didn't think she'd do a good job, so she wanted me to come talk to you. I'm worried about you, too."

"…Oh."

"I want to ask you something." She stopped dancing, just as the music stopped. Her silvery-white hair puffed out, then settled back down. Her blue eyes shone. There was a glow of sincerity in those sky blue eyes as she asked:

                    *   *   *

"Are you going to undo all of this?"
"Yes, I am."

He replied without hesitation. He couldn't lie to White Princess.

He'd made his decision. He would eventually go back in time. This moment would become nothing more than a dream. The time he spent here, looking at White Princess, holding her hand, would disappear without a trace.

She cast her eyes down slightly, but gave her answer without pause. "I see. I know you've made up your mind, so I won't say anything. But there's something I want you to remember." She squeezed his hands tightly. For the first time, he realized he was shaking. "Do you feel my warmth?"

"I do."

Her body was warm, and that heat seemed to melt his frozen body. It seemed a chill had crept up on him without his noticing.

She squeezed his hands even tighter and smiled softly. "Once you move away from me, this warmth will quickly fade. But it was there. Just like my feelings for you. The words I say may fade, but they were here. Nothing will change that, for all eternity. Never forget."

She gently twined her fingers around his, closed her blue eyes, and said with reverence:

"If something's important, it can never truly be lost. All of it will remain, inside you."

She tenderly rose up on the tips of her toes. Just as before, her gentle warmth touched him, then moved away. She had kissed him.

Kou quickly wrapped her in his arms. Everyone in the room was staring, but he paid them no mind. He simply focused on his next words, which he said with great care.

"I will never forget."

Even if he turned back time.
Even if these moments were erased.

He would never forget them.

"Never."

Outside, the snow piled higher.

After a while, a bell rang.

That bell marked the arrival of a new year at the Academy.

The Bride of Demise

12. THE DAWN PRINCESS

【Memories from the Beginning of the End: Isumi】

…Did I see any of this coming?

The hell I did. Of course I didn't see it coming. But I have a ton of
thoughts about it—and a hell of a lot of disbelief.

Still.

I'll listen.

…Cause he's my friend, you know?

* * *

Spring eventually arrived. The flowers were in full bloom, the wind
carried a pleasant scent, and the sun's rays grew warmer.

It had been this season when Kou first met Asagiri.

Soon, he and his classmates would be moving up a grade. He was
making good progress with Kashmar, who was slowly disclosing bits of
his research. For whatever reason, it seemed the king of the kihei was
lying dormant.

The situation remained stable. It might be that nothing would happen for some time.

Or so Kou believed.

And that's all it was—his belief.

*   *   *

Because one day…
…it came.

* * *

The first strike came without warning.

They were in the courtyard. Kou was with his usual group. They were hanging out after lunch. Mirei and Hikami were talking, Tsubaki was napping, Yaguruma and Kou were playing a board game, and White Princess and Black Princess were neatly doing each other's hair. Everything was peaceful.

That was when it happened—they saw a star in the sky.

"…A shooting star?" murmured Mirei.

The silver speck formed a tail in its wake as it landed in the Academy. The impact sent objects flying in all directions. A series of explosions followed.

Kou and the others didn't even have time to cry out. Whole swaths of the Academy were destroyed, one after another.

Kou just sat there, staring, eyes wide with shock. But at the same time, he understood. Many within the Academy had just lost their lives. It had happened so quickly it was hard to comprehend.

What's more, Kou realized something about the star that had fallen from the sky.

That's…

Something that appeared suddenly, that tried to destroy everything.

It was…

Could it be…?

"What's happening?" asked Hikami.

"I don't know!" said Mirei. "But we have to hurry and help everyone!"

Tsubaki and Yaguruma nodded. The students of Pandemonium quickly left Central Headquarters.

"Don't go near the fire! Head down the central road toward the main gate!"

"Hurry! But don't panic!"

Several students from Pandemonium were already helping evacuate the regular students. Others hurried toward the aftermath of the mysterious explosions. When Kou looked, he realized this second group consisted of Sasanoe and Crimson Princess.

Running over to them, Kou shouted, "Sasanoe, I'll investigate the explosions. Everyone else, concentrate on evacuating the survivors!"

"We don't know who the enemy is. You think you can manage on your own?!"

"Please!" Kou bowed without offering an explanation.

Sasanoe looked at him in silence. Eventually, he nodded and ran back in the other direction. Kou mentally thanked him before turning to his own Brides. "White Princess, Black Princess. I want you to help Sasanoe."

"What? Kou! You're asking me to part with my fate in such a situation?"

"Kou, you're asking us to let you go alone? I don't like that, not at all."

"Please! I have to go alone!" he shouted, the pain in his voice echoing around them.

The Princesses seemed uncertain, but eventually they nodded and rushed off.

"Fight well, Kou. I want you to call for us immediately if something happens."

"Luck be with you, Kou. Know that you can always rely on us."

Kou waved and watched them leave.

He was all alone now.

The destruction in front of him made the peace from before feel like a dream. He ran through it, and with every step he took, another scream rang out. The heat from the blazing fires singed his skin. He ignored it all, moving quickly to his destination.

When he arrived, he gently closed his eyes.

Then Kou Kaguro opened his violet eyes. But he hadn't gone back in time.

An intense light seared his retinas.

Familiar Academy sights were now shrouded in flames. The buildings for every major had been destroyed, and rubble was strewn across the ground. Even the café and shops located inside the Academy had been ruined and burned beyond recognition.

Central Headquarters alone, with its winged silhouette, just barely managed to retain its dignity.

In the distance, Pandemonium was leading the other students in an evacuation. There weren't many people still alive. A great number had been killed in the first wave of destruction. Even now, Kou could see someone's arm poking out from beneath the rubble. The air was heavy with heat and thick with the scent of smoke and burning flesh.

Kou Kaguro stood, unmoving.

He simply stared at the kihei in front of him.

It looked like a girl.

She stood in the Academy's square, her wings spread. Those wings, nothing more than an odd framework made from what looked like bones, clashed with her sweet appearance. There was a flash of blue light and a harsh, grating sound of machinery operating. But then the wings folded away in the blink of an eye, completely gone, and returned to her body as if they'd never been there.

She slowly blinked, then looked toward Kou. She stretched out her hand, like she was asking him for something.

He didn't respond. Silently, he readied his sword.

A building somewhere crumbled, and the fire gathered strength.

Wreathed in dancing crimson flames, the girl lowered her gaze. Her lips slowly parted, and she said, "I wanted to be with you forever. I wanted to be by your side forever. But that wasn't enough… This is my resolve. This is the proof of my love. This is the twisted manifestation of my desire. This is my…my…"

There, her words faltered for a moment. Her wings flew open once again.

The resulting burst of wind swept through the encroaching flames, sending a ring of crimson rushing into the air.

Surrounded by that dreadful sight, the girl closed her eyes.

Like a prayer, she whispered, "…This is my dream. My name is Dawn Princess. My alias is Grand Guignol."

Just like a princess in a fairy tale, like a witch in a fable, the awoken girl made an oath.

"Even if you don't want it, don't ask for it, don't accept it, I shall be by your side for all eternity."

"...I refuse," came Kou's simple response.

The girl smiled as if she'd known he would say that. Her smile was tender, filled with childlike innocence.

She continued to smile as countless people died around them.

She looked beautiful and cruel, horrifying and comical. But most of all, she simply looked heart-achingly alone.

* * *

He spoke to her. His words were filled with so much emotion it hurt.

"...Why?"

Why did this happen?
Why had it come to this?

His voice was steeped in confusion and regret.

"...Why, Asagiri?!"

Asagiri didn't reply.

She simply continued to smile.

She looked like a goddess.
And at the same time, like a simple, foolish girl.

The Bride of Demise

13. THAT'S RIGHT, I . . .

【Memories from the Beginning of the End: Asagiri】

I didn't ever think this would happen.

But he said we should, and that's all that matters to me. I don't care about anything else. That's why I'll go with him. I'll do my best to help him. Because that's what I want to do.

I love him, you know.

I really, really love him.
That's why I'm not afraid at all.

* * *

"Because I wasn't special, there was something I could never get." Asagiri stood in the center of the growing flames. She no longer looked human. She'd been completely changed into a Princess. Moving her bone-like mechanical wings, she spoke in a dreamy tone. "Do you know what that feels like, Kou?"

"What happened to you? What did they do to you?"

"Someone told me everything. Before you told me anything. They said you were alive and had a Bride. They said she was special to you, and if I wanted to be special, too, I should become a Princess."

"Who told yo—?"

"It doesn't matter who! That's not the point!" she shouted. Somewhere, a building collapsed, and bitter screams cut through the air once more.

Kou felt dizzy as he thought. This was all Asagiri's doing. He tightened his grip on his sword, though his hands were shaking. He didn't let go.

Asagiri stared into empty space as she casually lifted her hands. She continued, almost singing. "The research into making a Princess has been going on for a while, I guess. But every single person failed, except me. None of them could handle having their body tampered with like that. The physical danger from the surgeries wasn't a problem. There was someone there who could heal everything perfectly. It was their brains that went all funny. But I survived. I survived for you, Kou. It was for you that I overcame everything. But then they wouldn't let me go outside. They said I was a valuable specimen for observation."

Asagiri laughed like it was funny. She really seemed to find it amusing. She raised her arms and spun around, like she was twirling in a field of flowers.

"So I broke everything and left... I guess I went a bit too far and damaged the outside, too. But oh well."

"Oh...well?"

"Don't you see? I put up with so much. So much pain, so much hurt. All so I could be worthy of being by your side, Kou. I am Dawn Princess; my alias is Grand Guignol. That's my name. I'm a new living weapon. So, Kou, what do you think?"

Asagiri stopped moving and puffed out her chest proudly. It was like she hadn't heard Kou's rejection just before.

Cheerfully, innocently, she asked, "Am I amazing?"

"You were much more amazing before," replied Kou without pause.

Asagiri's chestnut-colored eyes clouded over. Her lips moved without saying anything. She was mouthing the words "It's that girl." She seemed possessed as she shook her head from side to side. "I need to kill that girl, don't I? Where's White Princess? I have to kill her right now!"

"This has nothing to do with White Princess! Asagiri, I never wanted you to become a Princess!"

White Princess and Black Princess were currently in Sasanoe's care, but both might come to him at any moment. He needed to finish this before that happened. But... *What does "finish this" mean?*

Stopping her?

Okay, but how?

Killing her?

Kill the friend who saved him?

Could he even make himself do that?

"Kou, why?" asked Asagiri. "Why won't you accept me even though I'm special now? ...Oh, that's it. You're afraid. It's okay, Kou; I won't kill you! I'll be with you forever; I'll protect you! I'll be with you, instead of that girl. I'll kill anyone who tries to hurt you! So—so...!"

Asagiri smiled, a smile that said he didn't have to be afraid of her. A smile filled with true pleasure.

Kou was filled with despair. He felt helpless. He couldn't think of a single word to persuade her.

That was when he heard a hollow voice, a voice that didn't belong here.

"..Asagiri, is that you?"

And Kou knew.

He knew there was one other person who hadn't run from the flames and the tragedy. After leaving the half-destroyed school buildings, that person had wandered, searching for signs of someone who wasn't there.

But then he had found her.

The person he loved.

"...Isumi." Kou turned back to look.

And there stood Isumi Hiiragi, bound up to his elbows in restraints.

* * *

"Asagiri... Asagiri, it's you! You're alive!"

"Isumi... What's on your hands?" asked Asagiri in surprise. She ran over to him. Concerned, she touched his arms. Her fingers snapped the chains holding the two arm restraints together. Isumi reached out his hands, now free, and hugged her. He wasn't afraid at all.

Asagiri blinked several times, her eyes wide with surprise. "Isumi, what's this about? What's wrong? You're acting weird."

"Thank God... Thank God... You're alive. Thank you, Kou... It's just like you said! Oh, thank you!" Isumi smiled.

Then Kou realized something. Isumi didn't notice anything odd about this situation. Kou was about to tell Isumi to back away from Asagiri, but he swallowed his words when he saw the other boy's joyous smile. Even if he said something, Isumi wouldn't hear him.

Isumi turned back to face Asagiri. Tears flowed down his face as he whispered, "I'm so happy you're alive... Because I love you."

"Love? Me? You—love me?" Asagiri spread her wings, the bone-like frame snapping through the air. She stared at him in a daze, then muttered, "Even after all these changes?"

"Of course I love you. I love you, Asagiri." Isumi seemed entranced. He stroked her cheek with a hand still inside its restraint. "That's why I'm so happy you're alive...," he said joyously, crying like a child. "Thank you, Asagiri."

"Oh... I'm so sorry, Isumi," she murmured, and Kou gasped.

What happened next unfolded in front of him in complete silence.

Then, within seconds, there was a dull sound as one of Asagiri's feathers pierced Isumi's heart.

* * *

Without withdrawing, she slit his chest sideways, dragging his heart out to hold it aloft. A streak of brilliant red trailed behind as she tossed aside the still-beating mass. It bounced across the ground, releasing a spatter of blood each time, before coming to a stop.

After throwing away Isumi's heart, Asagiri murmured, "I belong to Kou; I can't belong to anyone else. Saying you love me just causes problems."

"Asa...Asagiri!"

Kou rushed over to Isumi and pulled his body up into his arms, but the other boy was already gone. He still had the same smile on his face from when he had thanked Asagiri for being alive.

Kou bit his lip. Despair, anguish, and rage stained his heart black.

Asagiri stood before him, laughing. But as she sneered, she cried.

"Huh... But why? Why? I didn't have to kill him... Isumi was my friend, wasn't he? He became...my friend. Why? Why did I kill my friend?"

She pressed her hands to her forehead, and her fingernails dug into her face. Drops of blood ran down, followed by heavy tears.

She was panicking, still muttering. Her words kept coming, like she'd been broken. "Why…did I kill so many people…my friends? I wanted to be special. I'd do anything for that. But why? Why kill people? I'm a weapon. Is it because I'm a weapon? Because this is what I was made for? But why? Why Isumi? Why?"

"Asagiri, calm down; you're—"

"This is my resolve. This is my dream. This is the twisted manifestation of my desire. This is my…my…my? I thought… Aaaaaaaaaaaaaaaah!"

Asagiri screamed. Blue light flashed from her wings. It cut through the square and set even more buildings alight, destroying them.

She shook violently. Her wings started to change behind her. There was a creaking as the bony framework of her feathers spread even wider, and Kou knew. She was about to start a terrifying rampage.

This time, Asagiri would destroy everything for certain. Tears streamed down her face. She cried like a little child.

"Aaaaaaaaaaaaaaah! Kou, nooooooooooooooo!"

"Asagiri!"

Kou leaped up.

And he did what he had to do.

* * *

Kou's thoughts turned back to the day of the entrance ceremony.

"You're sweet."

"I just thought it'd be nice if I could help a bit. I don't think that counts as being sweet," replied Kou, and the girl smiled. Then she told him her name.

"I'm Asagiri. Asagiri Yuuki."

The two of them had been friends ever since.

And when death should have separated them, he remembered the sight of the flower petals at the ceremony and Asagiri's smile.

Now, held in his arms, Asagiri lay with a sword piercing her chest.

"…Is this your answer, Kou?" she asked in a daze.

"…Yes, it is" came his brief reply.

Drops of blood fell. It was Asagiri's blood soaking his arms. The strength drained from her wings, and their bony frame began to crumble.

Asagiri gently laid her head on Kou's and whispered.

"Oh. It looks like I've been rejected."

That was the end.

Asagiri Yuuki lay against his chest, her eyes closed as if she was savoring the moment. Kou cried and hugged her body to his own, his arms wrapping tightly around her.

She was gone.

And that was how Isumi Hiiragi and Asagiri Yuuki died.

The Bride of Demise

14. SHE JUST WANTED TO SAVE PEOPLE

【Memories from the Beginning of the End: Kurone】

...I don't have anything left to say.
I just hope my dear students find happiness.

* * *

He still hadn't decided precisely how far back he should go. But Kou Kaguro concentrated. Then he closed his eyes—and opened them.

He'd gone back to just after he met Isumi, to when he was researching in the library.

In that moment, he set in stone the deaths of the two Flower Rank students killed by the king of the kihei. But Kou didn't have the capacity to care about that. His mind was like a burning vortex consumed by a single possibility.

...*What if...?*

He rushed between the heavy wooden bookshelves, eventually reaching the one that held a collection of newspapers published in the capital. He looked through paper after paper, before finally coming to a conclusion.

Last time, his next move had been to go to the capital with Kagura. This time, though, he didn't wait for Kagura to arrive. He ran off, ignoring the attention he drew from the library workers. Putting the library behind him, he continued on to Central Headquarters, where he burst into the guest room used by faculty during their time off.

Kurone looked up. She had been stroking Green Princess's hair. Surprised, she asked, "What is it, Kou? Why did you come flying in here? You're making your mother worry."

"I have something I need to ask you."

"What's that?"

She cocked her head in confusion.

"Where did you take Asagiri Yuuki?"

Kurone froze instantly. Kou fixed her with a glare.

Something Asagiri Yuuki said had caught Kou's attention. "There was someone there who could heal everything perfectly." There weren't many in the empire capable of that level of healing magic. But there was one, just one, close to Kou and the other students. Kou had also seen her express disagreement with the ideology of the Coexisters. More than that, she believed kihei were to be used as weapons.

But what made him certain was that the disappearances had started at the exact same time as Kurone Fukagami's return to the Academy.

She was involved in the human experiments. And she wasn't just anyone—she was a major player.

Kou was sure of it. His eyes stayed fixed on Kurone.

Eventually, she started to move again. She nodded gently. First, in a kind voice, she said, "Making a scene here will only cause a disturbance. Shall we go outside?"

He followed her out into the hallway. She hadn't bothered to deny his allegations, but neither did she attempt to flee. She simply continued to walk ahead of him.

"Green Princess sent out a signal… We'll wait until White Princess and Black Princess can join us. You have that right." She said this despite the disadvantage it would put her in.

Eventually, the two Princesses came running. With confusion on their faces, they addressed Kou. "Kou, I got a message that you called for us…," said White Princess. "What's wrong?"

"Kurone Fukagami… She… What does this have to do with her?" asked Black Princess.

They lined up at Kou's side, frowning. But Kurone didn't offer any explanations. She just bid them to follow and walked off.

* * *

Kurone moved deeper into Central Headquarters. Once they reached the deepest part, where the walls gave way to relics of the prehistoric period, they came to a stop. Kurone pressed her fingers to a spot on the wall. Her biometrics were verified, and a hidden door opened.

She stepped down the stairs inside.

Eventually, they came to a small room. The shelves were lined with books on magic research, but this room wasn't like Kashmar's opulent laboratory. This felt more like a tidy office. Kurone poured boiling water from an insulated jug to make tea.

After setting out several cups, she said calmly, "It's real tea, and I haven't poisoned it. Drink up first, then we can talk. If you're not satisfied with what I have to say, we can fight. There's a room next door for combat trials. We'll use that."

"...What are you trying to do?"

"You have complaints about my conduct, don't you? I have to acknowledge any disapproval from Pandemonium. Everything I do is for you students and the Academy, even the experiments."

"For us?" Kou frowned. He hadn't expected that.

Kurone nodded gravely and, in a mild tone without shame, said, "Sacrifice the few for the good of the many. That is what my research does. More than a hundred people go missing from the Academy each year; many of them die. I merely use a few of their number to increase our options for fighting back against the kihei. That is the surest way to reduce the overall number of casualties. We must have powerful weapons in order to protect people. I want to create a system that doesn't need Pandemonium, doesn't need to use children as shields."

After speaking, she elegantly lifted her cup and sipped her tea.

Once she'd finished, she shook her head. Her next words sounded like a confession. "I don't believe I've made the wrong decision. But there are people who have the right to kill me. The girls whose warped thoughts and desires I used to try to make them Princesses, as well as the people who loved them. They're the only ones who have the right to stab me in my gut."

Kurone looked at Kou like she was measuring him up. He returned her gaze coldly.

She must have seen that his hatred for her hadn't changed. She smiled. "You are Asagiri Yuuki's friend, aren't you?"

"I am."

"Despite the perverse love she feels for you?"

"That doesn't change anything."

"I see... In that case, are you going to kill me?" She made it sound like the two of them were just chatting over brunch.

Kou was silent, but after a few seconds he gave a firm nod. "I am."

"I understand. Then let's fight to the death. Come, Green Princess," she said, calling to her Bride. Kurone slowly stood up and moved to the room next door, taking Green Princess with her. Then she murmured something.

"I had so hoped not to use my dear girl for battle."

She must have really meant that. She sounded sincere.
But Kou pretended he hadn't heard her.

* * *

The walls of the combat room appeared to be made from a single block, with no visible joints. It was massive, and the gray stone of its walls glowed faintly. They stood at one end of it.

Kurone moved without hesitation. She pressed a part of the wall, and a red light turned on, followed by the sounds of people walking in the distance. The sounds eventually stopped, and Kurone turned back to face Kou and the Princesses.

"Now we don't have to worry about anyone disturbing us," she said. "Shall we fight?"

"What did you just do?"

"I ordered the employees who help me with subject recruitment and research to leave temporarily. You don't intend to involve them in this fight as well, do you?" she asked.

He shook his head, thinking. He did intend to kill Kurone, but he wasn't entirely set on it. If she returned Asagiri and stopped doing the experiments, then there would be no need for him to kill her.

But as if she had read his mind, she shook her head and said, "You're a kind boy, but that won't happen, Kou. This is the only time I will allow you the right to kill me. I also have no intention of returning Asagiri. Our convictions must clash and come to a resolution. That's what I want, at least."

She smiled. There wasn't any inherent need for her to fight him. She could've feigned ignorance of the experiments, then had him secretly assassinated. But that wasn't what she had chosen.

Kou accepted her decision and waited for her to make a move.

Slowly, she walked toward the center of the room.

White Princess and Black Princess spread their wings. Green Princess stayed where she was.

With a fluid motion, Kurone opened her satchel and took out several syringes. She smiled and said, "Oh, and you shouldn't let your guard down. I'm confident I am more powerful than at least your other teacher, Shuu Hibiya."

Her tone remained gentle as she stabbed the needles into herself. The muscles around her neck bulged, then her entire body began to writhe. Just then, Kou realized something—Kurone's body was already modified, and she had just flipped a switch inside it.

"Kou, this—"

"Yes, I know," he said, watching Kurone's human form disappear. The person known as Kurone Fukagami's humanity had been lost. "This is something I have to kill."

The transformation ended quickly.

In front of them now was a massive living weapon, likely developed from research on the Babies.

* * *

"First, I'll burn it."

"Yes, and I'll tear it open."

White Princess and Black Princess emitted blue and black light, which easily cut into the Baby.

Fountains of blood erupted, but the wound immediately sealed up. This was Green Princess's recovery ability. They'd have to kill her first. The moment that thought crossed his mind, Kurone reached out a bulging arm to try to engulf her.

"No!" White Princess flew through the air and reached for Green Princess. Just before her hand touched the other Bride to rescue her, Green Princess slapped it way.

"Mother, I will always be with you," she whispered, enchantment in her eyes.

She moved forward and was absorbed into the mass of flesh.

With that, the flesh grew larger. Blood vessels rushed through the air and tried to snatch up the Princesses. White Princess used her mechanical wings to cut them, while Kou took one of White Princess's feathers and slashed more approaching vessels.

But soon they realized they were in trouble. The moment they cut into the growing flesh, it regrew. This was Green Princess's power. She had been engulfed, and now she was healing Kurone from the inside.

The flesh grew without limit. The floor and ceiling of the combat room were sturdy, and if things kept up like this, Kou and his Brides would be crushed to death.

"Kou, your blood!"

"Got it!"

When White Princess called to him, Kou bit his finger and dripped several drops of blood into her mouth. She received it like a kiss. Her light turned black and exploded over and over. She managed to gouge deep into the mass of flesh, but she wasn't able to burn it all away.

It squirmed and continued to grow, like a living manifestation of her all-consuming greed, for which she would even sacrifice her own kind.

From inside, several human figures emerged. They reached out to Kou and the Princesses, as if trying to embrace them. The flesh called, beckoning them to come, telling them how much easier it would be if they gave in.

It was like the mother of all living things. Listening to that wordless voice, a shudder ran up Kou's spine. Everything Kurone said came from a place of kindness. She was trying to kill him because she understood the pain he felt.

But he couldn't listen to her.

"I won't die. I'll kill you!"

The wave of flesh surged. White Princess wrapped her arms around Kou and leaped into the air. Black Princess came up beside them and said with regret, "Kagura has forbidden me from using my true power. However, he will allow me to unleash it in one case only—when Pandemonium is in great danger and when every member can be protected... This situation does not fulfill those criteria. I'm sorry, but I can't use my power. It's bound by his magic."

"Don't apologize, Black Princess," said Kou. "Kagura made the right choice. We'll just have to figure something out." He cut at the flesh as they flew closer to the ceiling.

The rapid growth didn't stop. It expanded faster than they could gouge it, burn it, or destroy it. Countless embracing arms reached out for them.

And then it happened.

"Time for the heavy hitter to take the stage."

A casual voice rang through the air. Black feathers danced before Kou and the Princesses. Then they quickly poured down into the flesh, bursting it open.

There was a series of precise explosions. The human forms growing out from the flesh screamed.

Kou and the Princesses turned in the direction of the voice, wondering what was happening. Someone was there, near the entrance.

His coat fluttered, and in a joking tone he said, "I always thought something was fishy about your goodwill-for-all attitude. Good thing I put a tracking device on Kou when you came back, Kurone Fukagami. Now I've got you."

There was a sharp sound as the feathers spiraling around him tore through the mass of flesh.

"Hope you don't mind if I, Kagura, the most powerful teacher of Pandemonium, jump into the fray."

*   *   *

It was the other Kou Kaguro.

Kagura had arrived.

* * *

"I'll shift the world out of phase if I keep going. You guys are still the stars of this fight. And I can't remove Black Princess's bindings—it'd make things dangerous later. But you can do it anyway. You've got the most powerful help, after all…Kou Kaguro," said Kagura. There was no concern in his voice.

He snapped his fingers and created a series of explosions. White Princess's blue light and Black Princess's black light pierced the weakened flesh. Kou watched their progress intently.

At last, coming to a conclusion, he called out. "The surface is expanding infinitely! We can't do anything unless we tear up the center. Kagura, can you keep shooting at a precise spot to dig a hole? I'll go inside with the Princesses. I trust you can do that much."

"No problemo," said Kagura. "You *are* asking a lot, but I'll make it look easy." He whirled his arm in a fluid motion, causing the feathers fluttering through the air to follow and stab into the mass of flesh. He kept up the explosions and used them like a drill to dig a hole deeper and deeper.

White Princess flew into the gaping wound, still carrying Kou, with Black Princess flying behind.

Kou's face was showered with a rain of blood. It was warm inside Kurone. It almost felt like being inside a womb. He felt an odd sense of comfort, despite the absurdity of the situation.

White Princess's sharp voice hit him like a slap in the face. "Kou, stay alert. There's something strange about this place. It's filled with viscous magic. I can't let you drown in it and be taken. You belong to me."

"I understand, White Princess." He nodded. "I'll make sure to stay focused."

The explosions continued. With each one, the flesh shrieked, but it wasn't a shriek of pain. It sounded more like delight.

They continued down the hole as it grew ever deeper. The farther they went, the more the flesh called to them. It tried to persuade them to stay. If they did, they would never feel pain or sorrow.

Something dawned on Kou. He had thought the infinitely growing mass was like a manifestation of Kurone's greed, but he'd been wrong. She truly believed she was doing all this for the students, for others. That's why the flesh was filled with the voice of her good intentions—and only her good intentions.

The explosions continued. Kou and the Princesses cut the blood vessels that tried to entangle them. Eventually, they came to a thin membrane. Kou raised one of White Princess's feathers and slashed through it.

A wave of thick blood surged out.

Inside, there were two people.

* * *

Kurone was there, unclothed, hugging Green Princess. They looked like a mother and daughter, simply lying there peacefully, their eyes closed.

Kou hesitated a moment. He took in a short breath. Then he raised White Princess's feather.

His sword fell.
And in that moment, Kou saw a vision.

* * *

There was a little girl lying down, wearing a white hospital gown. She wasn't a kihei. She was just a human. Only her hair had been turned green.

The operation was over. It appeared to be a success, but the girl fell unconscious.

The next time she opened her eyes, a long, long time had passed.

"Oh good… You weren't completely destroyed, were you?"

Someone looked at her and smiled. They had helped her when she'd been unable to activate properly.

That person was a woman, and she was kind. She was like the mother the little girl had lost. She stayed by the girl's side until she was able to move entirely on her own. She never got angry at the girl, no matter how troublesome she was. She was always kind.

And to the girl, she softly said:

"I want to save all children from the fighting. Would you be willing to help me with that?"

The girl nodded. Of course she would. The girl was proud of the woman. Even after she learned the woman was warped in her own way, she would always, always, be proud of her.

The two of them just wanted to save people.

* * *

"Kou!"

Black Princess's shout brought him back to himself.

In front of him, the mother and daughter slept. They looked so peaceful.

He gripped his sword.

He looked at the two of them.

No matter how beautiful their ideals are...

Even if sacrificing the few had been the only way to bring happiness to the many.

He thought of Asagiri's and Isumi's deaths.

He thought about the Academy in flames, his friend's tears, the cruel outcome.

He thought of flower petals at the ceremony.

And of Asagiri's smile.

He squeezed the hilt of his sword. This was for them.

*   *   *

"…I'm sorry."

And Kou Kaguro made his decision.

As he passed them, he swung his blade.
Kou Kaguro cut off the heads of the loving mother and daughter.

* * *

Blood spurted into the air.
Flesh tore, and organic components fell to the ground.

The woman who wanted nothing more than to save others was broken.

This was the result of Kou Kaguro's decision.

Kou and the Princesses flew through the collapsing mass of flesh. Their expressions were grim, their eyes fixed ahead as they hurried forward.
"I will not let Kou get caught in this… Not him."
"Indeed… Not Kou, never."
They continued on and slipped through a narrow hole. Spinning like a drill, they burst out.
Kou's tears scattered into the air.
The three of them were covered in blood, but they had escaped. They turned around to see the mass go limp, then dissolve and break apart. Everything that had been Kurone was now a deep-crimson sludge.
White Princess alighted, with Black Princess coming down beside her. They gently set Kou down on the floor.
Silence reigned for some time.
Eventually, White Princess whispered, "We did it, Kou."
"Yes… You accomplished this, Kou," added Black Princess.
"Yeah," he said.
"Uh, are you sure?" Kagura chimed in, and Kou's head snapped up to look at him. The teacher cracked his neck, then pointed out the door. "Don't you still have something important to check on?"

As soon as he heard this, Kou took off running. He sprang from the room. Probably due to Kurone's evacuation order, there were no employees around. He seized upon a large door nearby, located a handle for emergency use, and forced the door open. Inside, he found an unnatural room containing rows of liquid-filled vats.

Girls had been submerged in the vats. Kou ran through the room, checking the face of each and every one of them until he finally found the girl he was looking for.

"...Asagiri!"

He smashed the lid off, reached in, and drew Asagiri out. Green liquid sloshed over the side of the tank.

Asagiri was breathing, and it looked like she hadn't undergone any operations. Kou couldn't see any changes to her body, and there was no indication any of her organs had been replaced with organic components.

"Asagiri, Asagiri, Asagiri!" He shook her over and over.

Slowly, her eyes opened.

"Huh? Kou... Is that you? It's been so long..."

"Oh, Asagiri, I'm so glad you're okay!"

"I had a good dream... I dreamed I became special to you."

"You don't have to be special." He wrapped his arms around her. Suddenly, he remembered when he'd run her through with his sword.

But right now, Asagiri was blinking. She slowly returned his hug.

The two embraced in silence.

And so Kou Kaguro found his precious friend, Asagiri Yuuki, and brought her back alive.

15. THE FINAL ADVENTURE

【Memories from the Beginning of the End: White Princess】

Part of me…did suspect it might happen, that it might turn out like this.

I don't particularly care, though. Our hardships will likely continue, but I'm not upset by that; it doesn't make me sad. I simply respect my Groom's decision. I agree with it. After all, my Groom is the light of my world. That is all that matters.

No matter what changes, one thing will always remain the same.

I will always love Kou Kaguro with all my heart.

So long as those feelings remain within me, I will follow him.

To heaven or to hell.

Even if the world comes to an end.

We will always be together.

* * *

How lovely it would have been if the story ended there.

But for Kou and the others, there was a continuation—a continuation called life.

And Kou had a decision to make.

They were surrounded by blue light.

They—Kou, White Princess, and Black Princess—had descended to the tenth basement level of the central labyrinth. They fought their way to the location with the abnormal incubation nests they'd been to before. There was no one there. Kagura had already exterminated the kihei and destroyed the nests.

But as soon as they stepped into the room, the scenery before them shifted.

They had been forcefully teleported.

When they came to, they were inside the entirely white room with the long table. The king of the kihei sat there, a book written by a human laid out on the table in front of him. Kou didn't know where he would have gotten such a thing.

He smiled softly and said to Kou:

"Let's hear it, then."

"I'd like some information from you."

That was Kou's response. The king of the kihei nodded graciously. He looked at Kou and the Princesses like one might look at a naughty puppy or kitten.

The man's tender gaze irritated Kou, but he continued. "The other countries that used to exist... Were they really destroyed?"

"No."

The response was direct. Kou nodded; he'd suspected as much. The information he had been given as a student had been riddled with lies. It was hardly surprising they'd been taught a false history as well.

The king of the kihei leaned heavily against the backrest of his chair. He brought his hands together and whispered, "I'll tell you a little story. A story you might one day call the truth."

Kou yanked over a nearby chair and sat down facing the king. Then he listened to what the king of the kihei had to say.

Before Erosion... Imperial Year 25 BE.

The kihei abruptly appeared and attacked the empire, throwing humanity into chaos. Sixty percent of the population at the time was killed. Countless kihei invaded imperial territory. Contact with other countries was cut off, leaving the empire isolated. Ever since, they had been forced to fight a long and grueling war on their own.

Those "other countries" that used to exist had long ago faded from memory. The empire's independent magic research allowed the country to build impenetrable defenses, which, in turn, had led to the modicum of peace enjoyed today.

"But no one speaks of the time before... The Empire was at war even before we kihei appeared, you know."

The Empire was at a stalemate, facing off against three other nations. If the kihei hadn't appeared, it would likely have been destroyed. But with this new enemy, the war had to be put on hold. Ever since, the Empire had been forced to do battle with the kihei. Except that wasn't true, either.

"The Empire studied the kihei's abilities, and by taking the lost number five, they were able to regularly induce the Gloaming. This reduced the overall number of kihei, allowing the Empire to maintain control."

In other words, they'd never intended to end this long and grueling war.

To the Empire, the kihei were a powerful shield against their three adversaries. No matter how many casualties there were, the Empire never once thought about eliminating the kihei.

Even the students were nothing more than a calculated sacrifice.

What's more, if you were to pass through the areas inhabited by the kihei, you would find those other countries still in existence. They occasionally sent their soldiers to fight the kihei as well, but they struggled comparatively little. Even now, they must enjoy a degree of peace that Kou and the others had never experienced.

"Normally, the Gloaming would have occurred, and someone like me would never have been," said the king. "But once the Empire lost control of the kihei's numbers, I was created. Our battle with the humans will likely intensify. And on that subject, I have something I'd like to ask you."

"...What's that?" replied Kou.

"The Empire has betrayed you students from the very beginning. It seems that we are not your true enemy." He gently tilted his head to the side.

The Princesses glanced at Kou, whose lips were pressed tightly together.

Sounding genuinely amused, the king continued. "So then, what will you do?"

"I want to negotiate," said Kou.

The king smiled. He seemed to have expected this. He spread his arms and asked, "What about?"

Kou took a deep breath, then released it. He considered everything he'd seen up until now—the worst possible outcome, the decapitated heads, the truth of the world.

If he continued down this path, there would be no turning back.

With that knowledge, he revealed his decision:

"My friends and I will be leaving the Academy. I want your help."

* * *

The negotiations were honestly quite simple.

Pandemonium would stop killing kihei, unless they were attacked first. The king, meanwhile, would order the kihei to halt their attacks against Pandemonium as much as possible. If a kihei disobeyed the king's orders and went on a rampage, he would turn a blind eye when Pandemonium destroyed it.

In addition, he would help Pandemonium—who were a threat to the kihei—escape to a neighboring country.

"That is acceptable. As it causes me no harm, I shall honor your decision."

The king agreed to Kou's terms.

And so fate was decided.

Kou chose to abandon everyone except his Brides, Pandemonium, and his two close friends.

So that he wouldn't lose anything else that was precious to him.

* * *

Kou told Kagura everything. And then he informed him of his decision.

Kagura made a face that was hard to describe, but he nodded calmly. "Good. Soon, even the Academy wouldn't be able to contain Pandemonium. If there was another large-scale battle against the kihei, the Academy would try to drain you all dry… This is a good opportunity. You should leave. Will you be taking Asagiri and Isumi, too?"

"I plan to, as long as they agree."

"Asagiri will agree. After all, you'll be there. Isumi might be a bit harder… But he'll almost certainly go if Asagiri does."

"What will you do?" asked Kou.

Kagura smiled weakly and rubbed his neck. After a period of silence, he gave his answer.

"I'll stay. And if the time comes, I'll cross the border, by myself if I have to. For now, I still want to protect the regular students… Next, make sure you get permission from Shuu Hibiya." Kagura smiled. "After all, they *are* your second teacher."

And so Kou talked to Shuu Hibiya as well. He'd assumed they would oppose his decision, but surprisingly, they agreed.

"…I heard about Kurone Fukagami. The Academy's close to its limits. From now on, they'll be out to crush you. In that case, no one can criticize you for leaving on your own. But I'd like you to do me one favor. Please…take the Puppets with you."

"The Puppets?"

"As things stand, they'll just die like dogs for the Academy. Please get them out of here." As Shuu Hibiya spoke, their face was truly that of a teacher.

The biggest problem, however, was convincing everyone in Pandemonium. To do that, Kou would have to reveal his power. Once he'd decided, and with Kagura's help, he stood up before all of Pandemonium.

All of them—except the few who had been lost—looked at him, wondering what was going on.

Sucking in a deep breath, he prepared to tell his long story.

"…There's something I need to talk to you all about."

And so he began. He told them about his fifteen thousand repetitions through time and about the truth he'd learned.

* * *

"…Can you believe it?"

"Not one bit. Though, I sort of figured the thing about the Academy."

"I knew Kou was hiding something, too."

"Another country, huh? Sounds far."

"To be honest, I can't guarantee your safety," Kou said from where he stood behind the lectern. "But you're more likely to have a future there than if you stay at the Academy."

Kagura had made arrangements for provisions, and they planned to take along two spirits capable of automatic generation. They even planned to steal a transport vehicle, but they didn't know how far into their journey any of that would last. There was also the threat of the kihei.

A stir went through the members of Pandemonium. They began to debate the option Kou was offering.

But then a sharp voice cut through the commotion like a blade. "What do you plan to do about the regular students?"

Kou looked in the direction of the voice. There, he found a boy in black. Sasanoe, the one who had died at the hands of the regular students during the worst possible outcome of the festival.

"You are a Phantom Rank," he said. "We are those who lie in the dark to support Pandemonium and the Academy. I told you never to forget the pride that comes with that, Kou Kaguro."

His heels clicked on the ground as he walked over. Now he stood in front of Kou. White Princess and Black Princess started to move, but Kou held up a hand to order them back. He stared into the other boy's eyes, hidden behind the crow mask.

Then he said something he hadn't been able to say before. "Sasanoe, this Academy doesn't deserve your protection."

"Fool."

The strike was instantaneous. Kou was sent rolling across the ground from a punch to his gut, but he quickly stood. As Sasanoe closed in, Kou lashed out with a roundhouse kick. Sasanoe stopped the blow with one hand, then tossed Kou through the air. Kou flew upward, twisting his body and planting his feet on the ceiling. Then he pushed off.

Sasanoe grew larger in Kou's vision as he rushed downward.

As Sasanoe put his hand to his sword, White Princess screamed.

"Kou!"

"That's enough." Shirai stopped the liquid silver blade. Yurie, too, had stood up. The two of them looked at Kou with kindness in their eyes.

Stopped by his fellow Phantom Ranks, Sasanoe halted his attack.

Shirai addressed Kou quietly, "Hey, Kou. You're telling the truth, aren't you? If you're correct, we have the right to betray them. After all, they forced us to face the worst possible outcome. But this isn't about our rights. We are the most powerful, the Phantom Rank. If that is our only source of pride...then we can't abandon the regular students."

"Yes, that's who we are," said Yurie. "That's the only thing we live for."

"That's what I meant...fool," said Sasanoe.

Kou nodded in the face of their opposition. He'd had a feeling it would be like this. He'd known the Phantom Ranks would give this answer.

That's why he admired them so much.

Sasanoe watched Kou in silence. Then he said:

"You take Pandemonium away, then. We'll stay here and protect the students in your stead."

* * *

The Academy shunned the Phantom Ranks. They would likely end up dead in the long run.

But this was their pride. There was nothing else Kou could say to convince them.

Through gritted teeth, he said, "Okay. Good luck."

"You too. Don't die."

That was their last conversation.

With that, Kou and the Phantom Ranks parted ways.

They, to hold on to their pride and die.

He, to abandon his and live.

* * *

"I want to stay...," said Hikami, "but I can't let you guys go alone."

"I'll choose my friends," said Mirei. "I have no intentions of letting Kou and the Princesses suffer that tough journey by themselves."

"...To be honest," said Yaguruma. "I sort of figured the Academy was like that. I'll go with my friends."

"I have no interest in humans," said Tsubaki. "If Kou and the Princesses are going, then I'm going."

And so Kou's friends accepted his proposal.

It seemed the Puppets, too, had accepted Hibiya's. Helze sent Kou a formal request to accompany them. Asagiri and Isumi seemed to barely believe anything Kou told them, but Asagiri *had* been kidnapped for experimentation, and they ultimately agreed to go with him.

And so they all decided their fates.

* * *

On the day of their departure, Kou sat in the transportation vehicle.

Kagura had explained how to operate it, and Kou was now double-checking those instructions. As he struggled, Hikami came over

carrying boxes and began stacking various goods into the cargo section of the vehicle.

Kou called to him. "So what *are* you and Mirei in the end?"

"What are we? What does that mean?"

"Oh, come on, you know."

It might seem like the wrong time to be asking this sort of question, but Kou got the feeling that now, of all times, he had to ask.

At Kou's reply, Hikami looked embarrassed. Eventually, though, he nodded. "...Guess I'll be honest. I like Mirei. I feel something for her that's different from my love for my Bride. I want to be together with her, too. And actually, Unknown's already approved. If My Kitty gives the okay, I think I might just tell her how I feel."

"I'm sure he'll approve," said Kou.

That wouldn't change Mirei's and Hikami's hearts—hearts that loved their Brides above all else. If they wished to be together as well, surely their loving Brides would allow it.

"That would make me happy," Hikami said, nodding. Kou smiled.

"I hope it goes well."

"Thanks... Right, then. When morning comes, we leave."

"...Yeah."

"Do you have any regrets?" asked Hikami earnestly.

Kou closed his eyes and thought over his life up until that point. The day he met White Princess and she saved his life. The days he spent repeating hell fifteen thousand times. The worst possible outcome. Even during those harsh days, he hadn't come away empty-handed.

He was abandoning the Academy, just like the people whose heads he'd cut off. He was doing it for the people he cared about. For the futures of the people who were precious to him.

"I do have regrets. But there's only so much I can hold on to."

"And those are the things I'll live for."

Hikami nodded at Kou's answer. Once preparations were complete, Kou stuck his head out of the vehicle. The rough machine was currently hidden near the rear gate, cloaked with the power of a magic device. Kou stepped out into the road.

That's when he realized White Princess and Black Princess were looking at him. He waved to his Brides. Black Princess put a hand to White
Princess's back and pushed her toward Kou.

She and Kou stood facing each other. He took her hand.

She was the thing he most wanted to protect. He wanted to continue
to live with her, from now until forever.

With that hope in mind, he said, "Again, I vow. I give you my trust,
my adoration, my fate. This I swear, White Princess: I will protect you
for your sake."

White Princess leaped from the ground. She embraced him, laying
her cheek against his.

Like a parent cuddling a child, like a lover caressing their beloved.

And she firmly returned the vow.

"I shall be by your side for all eternity. I give you my restraints, my
servitude, my trust... This I swear, Kou: I shall kill any death that
comes for you."

The two embraced ever so tightly.
And with that, they made a promise.

Just like a real bride and groom.
Because they loved each other so earnestly.

Dawn would soon break.
And with it would come the beginning of a new—and final—adventure.

AFTERWORD

This marks the release of the third volume.

And as those of you who have read it may have realized, it is also the final volume of *The Bride of Demise*. There were problems with sales, and so I won't be able to continue the story.

You have my sincerest apologies.

But while we won't find out what happens to Pandemonium after this, I feel I did manage to reach some sort of tentative conclusion. I wrote a tiny bit more about what would happen afterward in a *doujinshi*, so please check that out if you're interested.

The story of *The Bride of Demise* would have become harsher the longer it went on. I'm certain that if I continued writing, several people would have died, so this is perhaps the best conclusion for the characters themselves. My thanks go out to everyone who followed Kou and his friends' fight.

I hope we can meet again in the next story.

Now then, on to my customary gratitude corner.

A huge thank you to murakaruki for the beautiful illustrations. You have my sincere gratitude for showing love to the characters of *The Bride of Demise*. Thank you to the project managers I and O, who I caused much grief. I, please take care of yourself. Thank you to my dear family, particularly my elder sister. Thank you to all the designers and people involved with publishing.

Thank you all so much.

Most importantly, I would like to thank you, the readers, from the bottom of my heart. We may have only gotten three volumes, but I'm grateful you followed Kou and the others all the way to the end. I can't thank you enough.

I pray their journey will lead to happiness.
And I hope that you and I will see each other again someday.

Keishi Ayasato

HAVE YOU BEEN TURNED ON TO LIGHT NOVELS YET?